Empathy

LITTLE SISTER'S CLASSICS

Empathy

SARAH SCHULMAN

ARSENAL PULP PRESS
Vancouver

First Arsenal Pulp Press edition: 2006

ARSENAL PULP PRESS
341 Water Street, Suite 200
Vancouver, BC
Canada V6B 1B8
arsenalpulp.com

Little Sister's Classics series editor: Mark Macdonald
Editors for the press: Robert Ballantyne and Brian Lam
Text and cover design: Shyla Seller
Front cover illustration from the Plume edition of *Empathy*
Photograph of Sarah Schulman: Bradford Louryk
Little Sister's Classics logo design: Hermant Gohil

Printed and bound in Canada

This is a work of fiction. Any resemblance of characters to persons either living or deceased is purely coincidental.

Efforts have been made to locate copyright holders of source material wherever possible. The publisher welcomes hearing from any copyright holders of material used in this book who have not been contacted.

Library and Archives Canada Cataloguing in Publication:

Schulman, Sarah, 1958-
Empathy / Sarah Schulman.

(Little Sister's classics)
Originally published: New York : Dutton, 1992.
ISBN 1-55152-201-2

I. Title. II. Series.

PS3569.C5393E48 2006 813'.54 C2006-900531-1

ISBN-13 978-1-55152-201-2

Contents

Preface 7

Introduction by Kevin Killian 9

Empathy 21

Appendices

"What I've learned about *Empathy*" by Sarah Schulman 191

"The Penis Story" by Sarah Schulman 203

Review in the *Los Angeles Times*, March 1993 212

Excerpts, "'A Person Positions Herself on Quicksand': The Postmodern Politics of Identity and Location in Sarah Schulman's *Empathy*" by Sonya Andermahr 215

Preface

Sarah Schulman's *Empathy* is a strange, funny, and disquieting book. Said to be lesbian literature's first foray into postmodernism, it is intentionally structured to be suffering from its own identity crisis. With wit and sophistication, Schulman toys with style in *Empathy*. Traditional narration and development of both plot and characters are rejected outright by the author, just as she rejects Freud's most dubious and regrettable theories. But even this rejection of Freud takes place within psychoanalytic sessions – one sweet irony among many. It is a calculated, but ultimately humane book, and Schulman's fierce intelligence crackles on every page. The critic Sally R. Munt once described the lesbian identity in *Empathy* as "a traveling implosion," which may be the simplest summation of this wonderful book.

Sarah Schulman is a tremendously gifted author whose books deserve regular revisiting, and we are pleased and honored to add *Empathy* to the Little Sister's Classics series. This edition includes an insightful and personal introduction by the writer Kevin Killian and in a new afterword, Schulman herself reflects on the impact of *Empathy* and the changes that have occurred since its release. Also included is a thematically related short story by the author and further complementary writings.

– *Mark Macdonald, 2006*

Introduction

Kevin Killian

"Now we may perhaps to begin?"

My copy of *Empathy* is battered, as though it's been field-kicked a couple of times. I don't remember kicking it myself, but the purply, green, black, and yellow jacket has lost a bit of its luster, grown faded and bumpy with use. I open it up, and inside the inscription returns, "For Kevin Killian and Dodie Bellamy, all my love, Sarah. December 10, 1992." That long ago! Dutton's edition was laid out entirely in boldface type, except the chapter headings, which were gray. Exactly the reverse of conventional printing style. A little disconcerting, as though asking readers, "Is everything backwards? Are the inmates running the asylum?" That *Empathy* is finally back in print seems to me one of the few just things that have happened in publishing.

Empathy was Sarah Schulman's fifth novel, and it delighted us – even those of us who had loved her previous books and wanted her to stay exactly the way she was, by virtue of an unabashed and offbeat formalism. By 1992, she had trained us to expect the unexpected, but still we were unprepared for the gleeful, mordant satire she offered up this time. No two chapters were anything alike, and the writing itself – its syntax, the connections her words make with each other – had undergone a sea change. It's the "acid test" by which I measure another's devotion to the art of the novel. Say it's a guy. He'll be jawing on about David Foster Wallace and Jonathan Lethem, Margaret Atwood and Orhan Pamuk, and I'll interject, "Yes, but what did you make of Sarah Schulman's *Empathy?*" Should he profess dislike – or worse, indifference, that indifference which must be the opposite of empathy – my mouth will maintain its smile, glinting brittly, but inside my soul coils with contempt, the low-lying radiation which poisons from underneath the skin, so that he moves away changed, an unknowing victim of the harshest test yet devised to separate sheep from goats. I see his innocent back, with my invisible knife in it, and like Marlene Dietrich at the end of *Touch of Evil*, I'm muttering at his gravesite, "He was some kind of a man. What does it matter what you say about people?"

I remember meeting Sarah Schulman at the poet Norma Cole's house, in Noe Valley in San Francisco around 1989 or so. It was just a cocktail party type thing, but as it turned out, became one of the signal events of my life. I had just finished reading *After Delores*, Schulman's deconstruction of the hardboiled detective novel, and it had plunged me into the splendors and miseries of New York's Lower East Side – its complicated women, its harrowing sexuality and pain. I had so recently finished reading it I had it on me at the party, and whipped it out to show everyone around me. You know the crazy things you do when you're awestruck. Norma said, "Have you met Sarah Schulman?" but I thought she was speaking in general, not in reference to the remarkably composed woman who stood in front of me, a glass of something pale and fizzy in her hand. She looked like a young girl to me. The kiss of youth was on her; it was hard to believe that already she had written *The Sophie Horowitz Story* (1984), *Girls, Visions, and Everything* (1986), and of course, my new favorite, *After Delores*. Maybe it was 1988 because as I say, I was carrying around that book like a badge, reverently, the way Bataille must have carried around the work of Laure.

When I met her, Sarah was dating the poet and filmmaker Abigail Child, and the two of them were living in San Francisco for a time, shooting a feature-length video they called *Swamp*. *Swamp's* premise is a simple one, though a host of farcical and apocalyptic events give it color and dash: the US has become so obsessed with keeping Mexicans away from its borders that it has turned all of Southern California into an artificial swamp. In an eerie parallel to later developments in so-called "Homeland Security," borderlands themselves must keep expanding exponentially, and soon San Francisco will be "swamped" over like all of the acreage to the south. George Kuchar plays an agent of the state who informs a bookstore owner that her property has been commandeered for patriotic purposes. "My shop a swamp?" she keeps crying, in shock. Carla Harryman, as the bookstore owner, in a little black dress with prim yellow polka dots, is the heroine of *Swamp*. When I found out that Sarah Schulman – *the* Sarah Schulman! – had written the script, I tried to get cast in the video. Why not? Everyone else I knew was getting their face in. I found out the number where Sarah and Abigail were staying and I kept calling, insinuating myself into the rhythms of their days and routines, offering to show them Kevin Killian's San Francisco, and boasting of my extensive acting career, which pretty much consisted of one-minute cameos in no-budget student films.

At the time, Sarah was hard at work on *People in Trouble*, the caustic, challenging ACT UP novel that was to change my life. For me, she came to embody the spirit of social change. "You must change your life," she said, like Rilke. It was a vision of reform, of revival, a wind of hope in a time of complicated misery. I had thought of postmodernism as a stateless thing, divorced from the political, and after reading her books I was never able to be so willfully innocent again. *Swamp* was made at the height of the AIDS epidemic, when ACT UP was still going strong, and though I think some of us saw it then as a bit of a relief from AIDS politics, when I saw it again recently I was struck by how fragile the city looks in it, how febrile and shakey. The poet and activist Tede Mathews, soon to be dead himself from AIDS, has a startling role as Steve Benson's mother, and when he's on the screen I have this weird sentimental attachment to him I didn't have in "real life." I finally landed a role in *Swamp;* I was Tom, an acclaimed, self-absorbed conceptual artist in the Vito Acconci/Matthew Barney mold. I sprang to fame with my expensive-to-stage, dazzling *coups de societé*; in one project, I suspended large girders from the ceiling of New York's Grand Central Station, and when a critical mass of homeless people had gathered beneath them, my computerized eye would release the beams and voilà! Instant fame, and I didn't even have to be there.

As *Empathy* begins, Anna is a young Manhattan office worker (temp division) having the sort of breakdown that leads to a total disarray of syntax. Doc, a street corner psychiatrist, lacks a diploma but works cheap and guarantees a cure within three sessions (just like latter-day HMO coverage). Anna's been rejected by a "handsome and wicked" woman who dismisses lesbianism as, if not pathological, then lacking the "fun" factor she can find with a man. Devastated, Anna plunges into her sessions with Doc, and eventually each winds up utterly changed by the other. American literature has had its "shrink" novels before, and to an extent *Empathy* depends on our vague knowledge of them, as we bounce Doc's apercus off similar doctors from the past. Dick Diver cures then marries Nicole in Scott Fitzgerald's *Tender is the Night.* In Sylvia Plath's *The Bell Jar*, Esther Greenwood succumbs to shock treatments. The narrator of Ralph Ellison's *Invisible Man* is tossed into a mental home for being a troublemaker. Most salient of all, in Philip Roth's *Portnoy's Complaint*, Portnoy tells his whole story to a silent psychiatrist, a tale so lengthy many readers forget that the psychiatrist is there. Dr. Spielvogel has only one line of dialogue, the last line in the book, so pointedly ironic it amounts to a shock ending: "Now we may perhaps to begin?" It seems to me that I remember Sarah asking Philip Roth to write a blurb for *Empathy*. *Portnoy's Complaint* is one of the books that Anna remembers from her parents' bookshelf.

Do those who write about psychoanalysis, even in disbelief, share a belief in the utopian world? If it's all about clearing away the underbrush so we can begin, what are we beginning? In Steinbeck's novels *Cannery Row* and *Sweet Thursday*, "Doc" is the helpful, thuggish scientist with the sweet side, who helps the down and outs manage their moonshine. Steinbeck's character is said to be based on his real-life pal, the marine biologist "Doc" Ricketts, who was married to a woman called Anna.... Reading *Empathy*, I also ponder the similarity between the shrink novel and the vampire novel. Anne Rice is always about the vamp's search for, and final encounter with, the older vampire who "sired" him. Here in *Empathy*, Doc's voyage leads him, finally, to Herr K., the analyst who "created" him – an eternally old Nosferatu of a doctor, more dead than alive, yet capable of a beautiful, unearthly wisdom and candor. "The sad reality is that people do not listen and do not take responsibility," the Doktor proclaims. "A lifetime in the office and in the laboratory have not revealed a way to change all that."

Empathy's thirty chapters alternate between Anna's point of view and Doc's complementary narrative. Our patient seems to draw strength as the analyst loses his perspective, indeed his connection to reality. This simple, effective structure is drawn from the plot E.M. Forster labelled (in his handbook *Aspects of the Novel)* the Thais plot, after Anatole France's creation. She, Thais the courtesan, becomes empowered as her protector loses his mind and soul to her. (I would call it the *Star Is Born* plot). One goes up as the other goes down: the oldest story in the world. In psychoanalytic terms, what happens is transference, then countertransference. At a certain point, the individual story of Anna becomes secondary, in Doc's mind, to his idea of her as a patient, then, as a woman.

Behind all this allegory stands the neo-Expressionist nightmare of *The Cabinet of Dr. Caligari*, or the harrowing rack of Ingmar Bergman's *Face to Face*, in which Liv Ullmann plays an analyst who descends into a madness queerly akin to sanctity. *Empathy* recalls the themes of several of Ingmar Bergman's films, and if you ever see *Persona*, themes of abandonment and defracted personalities will echo with your experience of this novel. If you name a character "Anna," is she bound by the code of narrative to become an analysand? In the post-Freudian age, there may be some readers who don't get Schulman's allusion to one of Freud's most famous early works, the *Studies in Hysteria* (1895), which he wrote with Josef Breuer, in which Breuer attempted to treat the "female hysteric" Anna O. The original Anna, strictly speaking, was never a patient of Freud's, but she has come down to us as shorthand for the way he (mis)analyzed women patients and chalked up whatever difficulties they were having in the world to repression of childhood sexuality. A few years before *Empathy*, British novelist D.M. Thomas restaged the Anna-Freud story in his 1982 bestseller *The White Hotel*, making them characters in a vast historical panorama in which, after Freud releases her to live a normal life, "Anna" gets caught up in the Holocaust and winds up a victim of the Babi Yar massacre. Applying a consonant strategy, Schulman is constantly moving her narrative out of the page, recontextualizing history, the very moment we live in now, so that her readers are snapped out of solipsism, and even the particular pleasures of reading a novel, to wake up and smell the brimstone.

"Now we may perhaps to begin?"

In Schulman's writing, behavior creates character. In *Empathy*, Anna says she has sought out Doc because she's never had sex with any lesbians, only with straight women and the curious. She's "never had a lover who let [her] meet her parents." Anna, like her palindromatic name, looks both ways, like Janus, at the horrid past and the impossible, burning future. She has a chance for happiness, but will she take it? Schulman's affection for and loving rebuke of Anna is typical of her character work. I now see that the character I played in *Swamp* foreshadowed one in *Empathy* – another of Doc's patients, the self-obsessed artist Doc calls "Cro-Mag." It's as if this particular character type was burnishing itself on Schulman's mind throughout this period, for he makes an appearance in *People in Trouble* as well. Cro-Mag's a real pig; he doesn't kill any homeless people in the name of art, but he would if he could figure out how to make a buck doing so. His gender – my gender – protects me as it does Cro-Mag from self-criticism, and indeed, neither of us will ever suffer from empathy.

Schulman's forte is language, I think more so than most novelists. She claims to have written only a handful of poems, if that, and yet poetry haunts the world of *Empathy*, like the modernist novel it most resembles, Djuna Barnes' *Nightwood.* Anna's abandon, as I have said earlier, leaves her vulnerable to sentences in a particularly lyric way, plunging the reader into a Baudelairean assault from page one. "Anna sat in the dark as the radio crackled like one emotion too many." Fine – I can almost see that; the static on the radio might resemble the mix of emotions she's feeling, although if she's in the dark she's not seeing, she's feeling, smelling, sensing. Next sentence: "Her passion was like sweat without the sweat." It's our job to picture this: is it a visual image, a tactile one, both or neither? It's an intellectual image which recapitulates *Empathy*'s larger strategies, calling into being a thing ("sweat") then withdrawing it and leaving behind the obverse of the image ("sweat without the sweat"). Meanwhile, as readers we're still grappling with the problem of how to reconcile the radio static sentence with this one. Reading makes a fetish of linearity, so basically we expect every succeeding sentence to modify the previous one. "It had no idea." What is "it" here – the radio? Anna's passion? The "sweat without the sweat"? In a conventional narrative, the notion of any of these potential referents lacking an idea would never arise. "It had no idea. No idea of what clarity is." That's a little different, a bit softer, not so black and white. Then metaphor arrives in a burst of brilliant lights, a series of stabs into the dark world. "It was two holes burned in the sheet. It was one long neck from lip to chest." Is it one, or two? Again, canny readers will realize at the end of the book that conventional number systems, the binary, no longer hold sway in *Empathy*'s expanded, hallucinatory landscapes. "It was one long neck from lip to chest, as long as a highway." I'm holding one finger to my lip, another to my chest, and trying to measure the space between them: it's nowhere as long as a highway, but that slash might feel endless to the person wounded. "Hot black tar, even at night." That's the metaphorical highway – or is it? It might be the roof of Anna's crumbling East Village building, where "a guy spits in the next apartment. There's a dog on the roof." The entire paragraph is only seventy-three words, yet it feels denser, more compressed, as though every word is being used at least twice, once for meaning, and again, for a higher, or lower, meaning; a meaning of a different register. So many have stressed Schulman's political and radical involvements that I think it worthwhile to note an equal or greater commitment to poetry, to evocation, to the domain of the word.

In another chapter, Schulman names the many varieties of silence in a bravura display of – well, it's the good old-fashioned Walt Whitman/Frank O'Hara "list poem." As I say, every chapter takes a different format, but in all of them I rock back and forth on my heels marvelling at Schulman's imagination, and her keen insight into every weird form of human interaction:

> When the phone stopped ringing she perceived a peculiar silence. One of many. Which one? There is a silence of perception. It wasn't that. Thoughtless silence? Forced silence? Chosen silence? Silence because you're listening. Fearful silence. Because the radio's broken. Hesitation. When you don't say it because you don't want to hurt the other person. Enraged silence. When you don't say it because it's not going to do any good. Waiting. Thinking. Not wanting to be misunderstood. Refusing to participate. Self-absorption. When a loud sound is over. Shame.

I wonder if this meditation could have come from a wish to expand on the enormously effective, yet somehow strangely prescriptive, slogan we then lived by, that "SILENCE = DEATH"? In another passage, Anna reflects that while "SILENCE = DEATH" may be true, "Voice does not necessarily equal Life."

Schulman's other forte is trendspotting. Born in the wrong era, she would have been an excellent practitioner of Mass Observation. "Doc's focus moved away from the hopeful and on to the fact that more and more people on the street were opting for nonfunction at an increasingly early age. So many men and women stick needles in their arms." These aren't facts per se, since they're reported from Doc's point of view, but they feel as though they've been observed. Anna considers options for success in 1991: HIV counseling, hospice work, teaching English to Russians. Trendspotting is Sarah Schulman's fingerprint, and you can see it running right through all her work. If, as has been suggested, Jonathan Larson was influenced by

People in Trouble while writing his musical *Rent*, for me the smoking gun is the detail about all the people synchronizing their watches to take their meds all at the same time. Nobody but Sarah Schulman would have commented on this, or even noticed the beautiful heartbreak of it. One might disagree with her social analysis, or marvel at how different life is on the Lower East Side than here in San Francisco, but like most people, I only notice trends when they jump up and kick me in the face. But just because she covers the big picture doesn't mean she has no eye for the telling human detail, the particulars. Indeed, the tension in her writing derives largely from her ability to sort of play each vision off of the other. Anna mourns the future that never came, the tomorrow promised by yesterday's futurologists. "The *Weekly Reader* had said that by 1990 she'd be flying around with jet packs. People would speak Esperanto and wear high-topped sneakers as they suited up for lift-off." Variants of these predictions do transpire in *Empathy*, but with significant differences. If not by jet pack, Anna does fly around, most notably on a nightmarish holiday to Djakarta, which she recalls in a soliloquy to Doc halfway through the book; it is *Empathy*'s single longest setpiece and, I think, the emotional crux of the novel. It's not just the East Village, or New York, or North America, that our lack of empathy has distorted to the point of madness; the divorce from feeling has infected even the most faraway, nearly "innocent" places. Anna's journey, accompanied by a thoughtless girlfriend, Lucy, comes in the middle of the book because, in classical epic, that's where the voyage down to Hell traditionally appears. "At the next table was a fashionable, clean-cut Japanese man dressed exactly like a fashionable clean-cut American man circa 1962. Only now that look has come back. You know, the nerd look. Tortoiseshell eyeglasses, khaki bermuda shorts, and white sneakers." It's so hot that sand stings through her shoes. "Kids were following us the whole time and I could smell my own flesh broiling." And everywhere they go, people tell them that Bali is "baguse," meaning cool. It's an Orwellian vision of language turned inward to fertilize a lie. In a world without connection, there's no in, and no out. There's no more there, thus there's no more here.

"Now we may perhaps to begin?"

I've had the strangest experience re-reading *Empathy* for the purposes of writing this essay. All kinds of feelings are returning, like the pins and needles feeling you get in your extremities after a long stillness. "Déjà vu" doesn't cover it. Late in the novel, two of Doc's patients, Jo and Sam, rehearse their *Virginia Woolf* neurosis in playlet form. "You're a hundred percent wrong, a hundred percent wrong, a hundred percent wrong." Reading this passage, I flashed on an evening fifteen years ago, when I created the part of Jo on stage in a bookstore in San Francisco during an evening of "Poets' Theater." This was the very same bookstore that was turned into a swamp by US federal agents in *Swamp*. Christian Huygen played Sam and I was Jo, and as you'll see, the play "Failure" begins with us kissing in the last minutes of bliss before a decisive argument. Our kiss lasted long enough for me to feel aroused and heady. We were directed to stay kissing until it became uncomfortable. And when "Sam" laid into me with his repeated, ever more vicious declarations that I was "one hundred percent wrong," tears stung my eyelids; I felt my face grow red in front of the whole room. I knew I was "acting," that Christian wasn't really my boyfriend, that he didn't hate me, and yet physics reached in and grabbed my ankles, knocking me on my ass. As the play reached its climax, I was shaking with grief, flayed. People in the audience clapped and cheered, but I only caught that on tape, much later; in the heat of the moment I kept quaking and blinking, my whole world torn out beneath me. And thus this little playlet might serve as emblematic of the apparently loose, baggy structure of the novel it wound up in. As you'll find out sooner or later, *Empathy* is in *portmanteau* form and contains everything but the kitchen sink (and in fact it does have a kitchen sink in it too). Is it a miscellany, pure and simple? If so, in this book (and in its equally excellent successor, *Rat Bohemia)*, Schulman found a way to bring life back to the novel, which in effect is the same as bringing life back to, well, life. Now we may perhaps to begin?

– *San Francisco, December 2005*

Empathy

Empathy is dedicated to David, Gloria, Helen, Charlie, Isabel, and in memory of Dora Leibling Yevish, born in Tarnopl, Austro-Hungary, on Rosh Hashana 1899 – died in New York City on February 19, 1982.

ACKNOWLEDGMENTS

I am very grateful to all my friends who gave me invaluable support during the development of this novel. In particular, I offer special thanks to Deborah Karpel with love and appreciation and to the following individuals:

Bettina Berch, Peg Byron, Lesly Gevirtz, Steve Berman, Diane Cleaver, Carl George, Lesly Curtis, Anne Christine D'Adesky, Jackie Woodson, Ruth Karpel, Ochiichi August Moon, Su Friedrich, Jim Hubbard, Kenny Fries (whose observations on the phrase SILENCE = DEATH are incorporated into this manuscript), Cecilia Dougherty, Carla Harryman, Bo Huston, Dan Carmell, Rachel Pollack, Laurie Linton, Betty Tompkins, my brothers and sisters of ACT UP, Jennifer Montgomery, Eileen Myles, Marie Dagata, Amy Scholder, Rachel Pfeffer, Kathy Danger, Beryl Satter, Julia Scher, and, always, Maxine Wolfe.

I appreciate the careful reading and specific comments that were offered to me by Dorothy Allison, Mark Ameen, Andrea Freud Lowenstein, Sharon Thompson, and Gary Glickman with a precision that was especially helpful.

For financial and business assistance I thank Tom Hall and the San Francisco Intersection for the Arts, the Cummington Community for the Arts, Sanford Greenburger Associates, Connie Lofton, John Embry and Mario Simon, and Dr. Irving Kittay for leeway in paying my dental bills.

I am very lucky to have had the opportunity to work with my editor, Carole DeSanti. Over the course of six years and three novels we have developed a resonant communication about writing and daily life that is uniquely meaningful for me. Her professional and imaginative guidance have been inspiring throughout.

Some of her intellectual attributes could be associated with masculinity; for instance her acuteness of comprehension and her lucid objectivity, insofar as she was not dominated by her passion.... It signified the attainment of the very wish, which, when frustrated, had driven her into homosexuality – namely, the wish to have a child by her father.... Once she had been punished for an over-affectionate overture made to a woman, she realized how she could wound her father and take revenge on him. Henceforth she remained homosexual out of defiance against her father.

– Sigmund Freud
"A Case of Homosexuality in a Woman"
1920

Prologue

Anna sat in the dark as the radio crackled like one emotion too many. Her passion was like sweat without the sweat. It had no idea. No idea of what clarity is. It was two holes burned in the sheet. It was one long neck from lip to chest, as long as a highway. Hot black tar, even at night. A guy spits in the next apartment. There's a dog on the roof.

In Anna's mind they were two scarves, two straps, two pieces of fresh pine wood. How many body parts can a person have? It's unfathomable.

MY SUGGESTION

ANNA O. *and the woman she loves are together in Anna's stark apartment. The* WOMAN, *handsome and wicked, is sitting in a simple chair.* ANNA *is standing coyly within range of her lover's arms. They refrain from touching.* ANNA *feels casual and pleasurably feminine.*

ANNA

I don't think it affects me, actually. I don't have any problem with it. Don't you believe me? Honey?

WOMAN

I believe you.

ANNA

You're very sexy to me.

WOMAN

Does that make you nervous?

ANNA

No, it makes me feel good.

WOMAN

Talk some more so I can watch your mouth move.

ANNA *looks at her inquisitively, wondering if that was an order. But she gets so caught up in the woman's beauty that the question gets lost.*

ANNA

About?

WOMAN

About romance and … a car.

ANNA

A car and a lover and a loud radio. The top was down. The sun was bright. I drove with my left hand and got her off with my right. I felt her come in my hand as I was speeding and I remember thinking, *This is love. This is fun*. Then we pulled over and laughed. I was so comfortable.

WOMAN

Happy.

ANNA

Yes. Relaxed. More?

WOMAN

Tell me about a mistake you made. A big one.

ANNA

A mistake?

She hesitates, surprised.

ANNA

Wait.

WOMAN

What are you doing?

ANNA

I'm looking to see if I can trust you.
(*Looks*)
Yes, I trust you. I met a woman and a man and we got too close. There was the inevitable night of drinking and teasing until we decided to play a game.

WOMAN

At whose suggestion?

ANNA

My suggestion. We decided that each one would say their fantasy and the other two would fulfill it.

WOMAN

Uh-oh. I don't do *that* anymore. So, the man went first …

ANNA

The man went first and he wanted us to …

WOMAN

Make love in front of him.

ANNA

No, not so easy. He wanted his dick in our mouths. Then it was Joanie's turn.

WOMAN

And she wanted you to get him off.

ANNA

Of course she knew I hadn't fucked a man in about eight years, but she wanted me to climb on top of him and fuck him. And I did. No problem, like I said. I have no problem with it.

WOMAN

Then it was your turn.

ANNA

I said I wanted Jack to leave the room and I wanted to make love to her, but she said no.

WOMAN

No?

ANNA

She refused. Now what do you want me to do?

WOMAN

There's this peach slip that has been under your dress all evening. Let me touch it.

ANNA O. *takes off her dress and stands in front of the* WOMAN *in her slip. The* WOMAN *touches it.*

BLACKOUT

Later there was a whipping in a hotel room. That woman made her pay a dollar before she let her come. There was sex in a telephone booth, on the pier, in a public bathroom. She kissed her with someone else's pussy on her breath.

Anna walked to the end of the bedroom and looked out the window through the hot iron gates. She walked through the kitchen, dirty linoleum sludging underneath her feet. The cigarette was burning. She opened the front door to see a different kind of light. Someone was coming up the stairs. It was cooler in the hallway. The moon was red through the staircase window.

Up close that woman looked very different. She was still a princely beauty but she wore a rough, white, dirty, sleeveless T-shirt like some guy. Her nipples hooked its edges. The hair under her arms was black smoke, wire, a raccoon tail, dry polish.

"What's the matter?" Anna said.

"Remember that fight we had last winter?"

"Yes."

"Well, I was thinking about it," the woman said. "And then I finally realized something."

"What?"

"I realized that I'm not a lesbian anymore. I realized that women don't have fun together. I realized that that's not love. I realized that men are heroes after all."

As for Anna, she was caught in a burning apartment. There were flaming rafters and charred beams falling all around her. There was smoke choking her. But it had happened so fast she had not yet decided to flee. She was still, unrealistically, trying to determine which items to take along.

"What is your definition of a hero?" she asked.

"A hero is someone you can be proud of," the woman said. "To be proud of someone he has to be bigger than you so you can look up to him. You can feel safe when he is near you. Especially a man who has soft skin. When a man is near you who has soft skin, soft and sloping like a woman's, then you can feel safe."

"But he's not a woman?"

"No."

Anna did not want to understand. She knew this word *he*. She'd heard it before in every circumstance of her life. But what did it mean? What did it really mean?

"What is your definition of fun?" she asked.

"Fun," the woman explained, "is when you get what you've always imagined. When you've always known what you want and then you get it. With a woman you can't have this because you've never imagined what you've wanted. There's no gratification. No gratification at all."

"This is so brutal," Anna said. "Why is this happening to me?"

"Don't give up so easily. You're too weak."

"There's something very important that I don't understand. How can I be a woman and still be happy?"

"Shut up," the woman said. "Don't tell me what to do."

What are you talking about? Anna thought. *What does this mean about me?*

That night and for many nights to come, Anna could not sleep. Months passed and still she could not find peace. Finally one night, tossing and turning, she found herself in bed in the middle of an old-fashioned thunderstorm. Branches howled and scraped against her window. It could have been any lonely night in any storybook with one contemporary exception. Nowadays, when a lightning bolt hits, it sets off car alarms all over the neighborhood. That old reverberating crackle in nature is no more.

Some nights Anna flies away in bed. That night, awake in the dark, sheets of ice sailed between the stars. They flashed in the moonlight as her covers slid to the floor, as the secret was revealed. Anna's pudgy white body looked like diamonds between those sheets. Those crystal slabs of shine. But then the lightning flash set off car alarms and so Anna, interrupted, pulled the covers over her demurely supple flesh. Back on earth she lay, dissatisfied, between two pieces of printed cotton. Those sirens droned on all night.

What happened? she asked herself. *What just happened?*

Then a few other questions came to mind.

What happened to the world that I was promised back in first grade in 1965?

Not only had she been promised successful middle-class romance, but other treats had been mentioned as well, like the Jetsons, robots, and the metric system. In fact, when Anna was a girl, *The Weekly Reader* had said that by 1990 she'd be flying around with jet packs. People would speak Esperanto and wear high-topped sneakers as they suited up for lift-off. As a kid she'd bought a roll of aluminum foil and Scotch-taped it on her own chest to make one of those silver suits. Then she jumped up. Flying seemed desirable, something everyone would want to do. Before her lay a universe of neon Ping-Pong balls, as everything imaginable was endless. With a pixie haircut she played with the boys because towheaded American males were birds then. Those guys were rockets, superheroes, untouchable.

Anna turned over in bed, rain sliding down the window. She remembered the promise of an antiseptic future: domed cities and artificial weather. Somehow this was supposed to be good. Anna O. knew that hers was the last generation to believe the future would be better. Now, she feared the future. With that last thought Anna fell into a troubled sleep.

Chapter One

The next morning a doctor awoke from unsettling dreams. He spent a few indulgent moments luxuriating in the warmth of his covers before facing another winter day. This doctor was a young one. He was soft about the face and had clear brown eyes that exhibited a distracted kind of caring. He passed his hands over his small, fleshy body and then stretched his eyes and fingers toward the wall. The world was his this chilly morning. He could be human, inadequate, and still have it all.

Doc didn't have a PhD. He had never been to medical school. Yet he had spent his entire adult life working steadily as a street-corner psychiatrist. It was one of those occupations that come as a surprise, but once you think it over, street-corner psychiatry makes all the sense in the world. And he was the obvious practitioner because this doctor was always looking for his answer in other people. As a result, he was obliged to look for some hope within them too. He believed in change on a one-to-one basis and in that case therapy was a two-way street. Lacking a diploma didn't matter. And he didn't need to be able to prescribe drugs. His patients had enough of those already.

Doc was more than Freudian. He had been born a Freudian. His parents were psychoanalysts and so he had done his internship and residency simply by growing up. Doc had been raised in psychoanalysis much the same way that other children are brought up in a Protestant church, or communism. Of course, in some ways Freudians are a cult because they have both a reductionist vocabulary and a spiritual leader. They do not have universal appeal. Like all structuralists, Freudians have a system of thought that explains everything. However, the reason Doc felt more akin to Episcopalians than Scientologists was that despite their limited numbers, Freudians have managed to penetrate culture and affect it in silent and unspecified ways. They have managed to be bizarre but seem objective.

Throughout his life the doctor had slowly unpeeled and discarded the burdens of a Freudian worldview. But the job was only half done. Like an ex-Catholic who can't stop confessing, the sense of transgression always lingers. Through a system of logical considerations and accumulated life experiences, Doc was able to let his family religion slip through his fingers. For example, he did not give his own parents power over everything. They were often bewildered themselves and made mistakes. Doc and his father had the same way of sitting and listening with expressionless concern. They both waved their arms about broadly as the substitute for a feeling. His mother and he were wildly opinionated and would have been happier in some mass movement somewhere made up of people with hope.

Another Freudian idea that Doc had abandoned had to do with meaning. He knew that some acts were completely without it. There are things that actually just happen. A third disagreement came in his understanding of sexuality. As hard as Doc tried, he simply could not imagine a way that it could be changed. All you could do was make someone feel bad about it. Finally, after staring at many therapists around the dinner table, Doc had concluded that transference was just another kind of love – no better or worse than the most ordinary romance.

Still, he did retain one fundamental orthodox concept that had grown into the foundation of his personality and belief system. The doctor maintained that there were *reasons* for behavior and those reasons could be identified. He believed in the big *Why*.

As a result he had a very unhappy life. Whenever he found that someone he loved was hurting him or being hurt by him, he would try to discover *why*. He would ask, *why*? But most people don't want to know why. They just want to keep doing it. Doctor had lived long and loved many and he knew that this was true and would always be true. But he could not accept the silence. So, he gave up on love and went into business because it was more important for him to understand than to have someone to go on vacation with.

Once, Doc and a woman had gone for a walk. It was near Christmas and all around them Christians were spending money. It was exciting to watch their desperation. Doc and his friend walked slowly as the Christians panicked, wildly stampeding like llamas with the alpaca still on them. The two of them turned down a side street looking for a bookstore where more sedate worshipers would be buying Robert Frost. There, they saw a store window, fully decorated, with no observers. In it was a pyramid of ice. In the ice, forming a pattern by their various locations, live lobsters had been planted tail first. Their claws were stuffed with bright ribbons and wildflowers. As they waved about, struggling to free themselves, the flowers waved too, creating a living ice garden. It was really beautiful. Overcome with the romance of the moment, Doc turned to his companion and said:

"You are the woman I want to have in my life. I can talk to you and about you at the same time. That is why I will always love you."

A great burden was lifted from his chest then. He had finally found a woman to both love and analyze. But unfortunately this did not seem to her to be as valuable as it appeared in Doc's eyes.

"I'm going to get you," she said. "I'm going to outclass you in the minds of other people."

With that she fled, her white leather coat flapping in the Christmas night.

There was a whole relationship beyond what she said that night. She was concrete, not just some particle floating out there with Doc's other abstract ideas. When did he meet her? How long did they go out? How often did they see each other? He wanted to avoid the whole chronology. Instead, for the next few months he asked himself on a daily basis why she had been so cruel.

This woman in white leather was clearly an oppression experience. She could not be nice. Yet, to this day, Doc mourned, stupidly, the absence of her hostility. After all, being put down by her was still a relationship, no matter how feeble. Like most mean people she was equally self-centered and malleable. This fascinated Doc. Secondarily, there was something in that combination that reminded him of America. But much more important, he wanted a happy ending. He wanted some modicum of control.

Now, so much later and alone in his apartment, Doc did some self-analysis.

I'm not the kind of person for whom time heals. The only thing that heals me is resolution.

Doc would have no rest until he didn't care whether she would ever love him again. But God, that would take up so much of his time.

Time passes very slowly for me, Doc thought.

"This was an accurate perception," he said and then remembered, with a start, that it was his own life on the table. He had put his own self on the couch. Warily, he walked through the dark kitchen and shined a flashlight into the bathroom mirror. His face was obscured by glare and shadow. All he saw was one soft lip. He ran back to the bed.

Even though the doctor was young, he didn't feel that his life had happened quickly. He felt that it had happened very, very slowly and he fully realized the impact of years of twenty-four-hour days. This was why he hated the past. He never wanted to relive one minute of it. He couldn't even bear to think about it. He wouldn't even want to relive breakfast, because the doctor was waiting for a particular thing to happen. A particular explanation.

Enough reminiscing, Doc told himself sternly. *I could spend the rest of my life poring over the first thirty-one years of it.*

Finally he rolled himself out of bed.

At his feet lay yesterday's ancient drab clothes. They would do fine. It was easier to dress down when working the street. Frankly, it helped his patients trust him. They didn't worry about trying to impress. Doc spooned out a cup of instant coffee and ran the comb through his hair. Then, in a burst of impending entrepreneurial spirit, he went downstairs to take care of his own business before the Hare Krishnas got the best corner.

As soon as he hit Second Avenue, Doc started madly distributing his business cards to reasonable-looking neurotics. Anything to drum up new clientele. Since Doc had a policy of never seeing a patient for more than three sessions, he had to advertise constantly.

THE DOCTOR IS IN

LAY ANALYSIS MY SPECIALTY

RATES YOU CAN EMOTIONALLY ACCEPT

Plus address and phone number.

Handing it out with meaningful glances, Doc looked at passersby as potential patients. He wondered which person and their problems would enter and transform his life?

Doc noticed one young man who had that expression on his face as though he had given up looking for work. He couldn't stand his jobs, even the one wrapping muffins. Doc could see he was blaming himself, believing the lies on the television set. Doc could tell him how many millions had the same problem. That it wasn't personal.

Another guy passed by. He had a neuromuscular disorder, maybe MS. His boyfriend was scared, didn't know what to do. Doc could sit down with both of them and lay out the facts. He could help them face it.

That woman over there had an observant ego. Even though she was tired and on her way to or from work, Doc could tell she watched everything closely. Sessions with her would be a sharing of ideas, a place to freely engage. Doc and she would sit back proposing this or that. They would just talk.

These strangers filled him with feeling. There were so many things he wanted to go through with them. He wanted to love them. There was a palpable relief in being Doc. He felt suddenly happy, purposeful in life. Being happier let him see more. It put the present day in sharper perspective. Of course, that had its own side effects because then Doc began to notice the other Americans. He started looking around at all the sights one normally ignores. Doc's focus moved away from the hopeful and on to the fact that more and more people on the street were opting for nonfunction at an increasingly early age. So many men and women stuck needles in their arms. Doc couldn't even go to the post office without passing two or three on the nod.

He felt personally responsible. If only *he* could come up with a solution. It was up to him. Doc couldn't think of anyone else who could do it. *Some of us walk to the store*, Doc thought. *And some stand there drooling, slowly sliding. The subway makes speeches under our feet.*

When he finished his advertising duties for the day, Doc started wearily back toward home. There was so much bad news in the air and on people's faces. Recently someone had mentioned that there would be no more winters due to global warming and no more rain forests. But this year was as cold as it had ever been and so even some disaster news was called into question. Personal disasters, however, were everywhere in human form, lumped under blankets in corners or smack in the middle of the sidewalk, bleeding from the face with no gloves while the ambulance took forever.

"Hello, ambulance?" said Doc into a pay phone. "There is a white man, mid-forties, in a business suit. I think he had a heart attack."

It was the only way to get them to come.

"Are you sure it's not a homeless person?" the radio dispatcher said.

"Yes," Doc said. "He's wearing a watch."

It worked this time but even desperate methods were increasingly undependable because there were fewer and fewer pay phones that actually worked or that took coins and not just calling cards.

Every time it rained, Doc knew it rained on people. When it snowed, it froze them. There was no longer weather without imagining human objects. The cozy inside became an increasingly rare commodity and Doc was aware of this all too well. But even with a substantial amount of knowledge, every day something big happened in the world that Doc could not fully understand. If there was a global economic crisis, where did all the money go? Was the money unreal in the first place, only now everyone finally said so? Or did a couple of people manage to grab it all? Just by looking out the window Doc noticed more news than there was room for and he felt curiously uncomfortable about people everywhere getting really angry while Americans stayed the same.

It happened to be Christmas again, which was always confusing because he couldn't help feeling certain feelings. Certain whimsies entered Doc's heart even though they had nothing to do with his own life. The public spectacle intensified at this time of year and, caught up in the display, Doc had a lot of opportunities to look around wondrously. New Yorkers are introspective in that way. They're the kind of crowd that pays attention to the crowd.

While observing this particular Christmas, he was struck most particularly by the Emergency Disaster Services Mobile Canteen that was parked outside the tent-city refugee camp occupying Tompkins Square Park. He wasn't sure which word surprised him the most: *emergency*, *disaster* or *services*. It was clearly a time for setting priorities, every American knew that. Should they choose preventative food on their plates or pay insurance bills for hospitalization that didn't exist? Of course, this was a middle-class dilemma. Christmas smelled sexy, like wet cheese.

Those three hundred homeless people living in the park across the way had certainly changed his life. Now, every night, the GPs, the Garbage Pickers, tore open every plastic bag and scattered its contents all over the sidewalk, looking for something. Every morning the sidewalk was covered. Also, people shit and pissed in crevices and doorways. This was especially true of the crackheads who had given up on certain elements of social training and drug dealers who didn't have time to find a bathroom. The whole sidewalk stank. Most difficult for Doc's own sense of personal integrity were the homeless guys with paper cups opening and closing the doors at various cash machines all over the city.

"You gotta tip me," one of them told Doc, as he pulled out his twenty dollars. "'Cause I don't have one of those cards."

"It's not the card that gets you the money," Doc told him. "You've gotta have an account. I mean, you can only get back the money that you put in there in the first place."

"You're kidding," the guy said, smelling awful. "I thought you just needed the card to get the cash."

That afternoon, Doc started counting and discovering that eight different people stopped and asked him for money. With each one he had to make a moral decision. But he didn't know how. He didn't know which set of values were applicable. If he gave each person some reasonable, humanly respectful amount, he wouldn't have enough for himself. If he gave each a token amount, they wouldn't have enough. Then Doc realized that even if he gave each person a reasonable amount every time they asked for it, this still would not help them. It would not get them off the street. He could not figure out the difference between right and wrong. So, he gave each one something.

Yes, it was Christmas and Third Street looked great. The Hell's Angels outdid themselves by being tasteful for a change. Their decorations were arty and conceptual in alternating geometrics. The whole block of tenements was draped in plain light, lush and dripping like kudzu. No Santas, Baby Jesus, or reindeers. The Angels dumped the kitsch and gave everyone frozen foam blossoms in green, red, and white. Of course, the Angels were bullies, and not heroes, so there was a vast complication to this beauty because Doc was dependent on vicious killers to get it.

Overwhelming news and overwhelming personal confusion. Plausible deniability, extreme money funneling, circuitous routes. Not telling people or telling people that you're not telling.

Face it, Doc thought. *From the first divided cell to the last pump of the respirator, a group of people is the most dangerous force on earth.*

Chapter Two

Anna came home from the temp agency early. They had promised to send her out but they didn't. What was wrong with her? It used to be that stockings, heels, and combing her bangs forward were the only prerequisites for employment. Now she had to know Word Perfect, too. Feeling inadequate and inappropriate, she splurged at the newsstand and then made a beeline home, running the gauntlet of beggars and people handing out circulars, business cards, and discount flyers. She clutched their offerings to her chest and ran up the stairs.

The first thing Anna saw at home were three roaches hanging out by the dish drain. Vengefully, she put out the *Combat* and waited. Those assholes at American Mutual were too much to take. Thank God she didn't have to go back there. In three days she had typed up all the correspondence pertaining to a group of workers with asbestos poisoning trying to sue the company. Then there was the puny executive who cornered her at lunch.

"How can you live with yourself knowing that you're fighting poor people who are dying from asbestos?" she'd asked.

"Most of them were heavy smokers," he said, satisfied, and then asked her out for the second time.

Later in the office the old Italian guy who had worked for the company for twenty-four years was moaning and groaning about some fag who'd moved in next door.

"What do you care?" Anna said, trying to be sweet about it. "He's not bothering you."

"Not bothering me?" the guy said, offended. "He's a big queen

How would you like it if some butchy woman was in your face all night long?"

There was no one to take it out on but the roaches. Now, as she walked through her apartment, there were black plastic squares in every room protecting her from vermin. But actually this gave her no comfort because she did not know how *Combat* worked. She had no assurance that it did not operate on the same basis as radiation, another invisible substance.

It was time to relax. But how? Anna had given up bicycle riding because her bikes got stolen every two months, and the price of bike locks was hovering somewhere near the cost of health insurance. She couldn't bear to watch television. She couldn't listen to most of what was on the radio because of the way the music constantly rhymed. But everyone has to give over their mind to some electronic field. Everyone needs someplace to surrender. Anna liked magazines. They were glossy machines. The only technology that she could fold. She read them on a regular basis because they were absorbing. Each one came out on a specific day of the week and was good for an hour of absorption.

Anna took off her shoes and left them standing in the middle of the room. She carefully rolled down her stockings, knowing that the slightest scratch would cost her. Damn it, they caught on a toenail. This was so humiliating. It made her sick to death of herself. Anna read *People* magazine. Why was gossip more interesting than the world? It had something to do with marketing, of that Anna was sure. It had something to do with the organized promotion of a Fake Life. As far as Anna could see, marketing seemed to happen to everyone: drug dealers, beggars, people with careers. It was an unacknowledged public embarrassment. That's why *People* was her private pleasure, not to be enjoyed on the subway in front of others. This week's photo had a picture of some guy. She glanced at the face but it was meaningless to her. The names on the cover were: CHRIS EVERT☆PRINCE RAINIER☆ZSA ZSA☆CHAPPAQUIDDICK

She was not interested in any of this. Thank God those names were timeless. They involved no commitment. It was like saying "but," "that," and "which." Prince Rainier was daily life.

More important than the stories were the advertisements because *People*'s articles tried to homogenize while the ads wanted to grab you. One said REORIENT YOUR THINKING. It was from Nissan. Behind the car was a glossy blue sea. The sea reminded Anna of those window displays with shreds of tin foil fluttering in the breeze of an electric fan. It wasn't sexy. The Japanese were people to admire grudgingly, but never strive to be. They weren't sexy. They didn't appear in their own ads. The car was enough.

Anna skipped to the video section, tried the movie section but had to skip it after reading one word. What were they talking about? She couldn't understand why they thought something was important. She couldn't understand the values. There was nothing in this magazine that she saw in the mirror. No person, gesture, slogan, or hairstyle looked like her. In fact, there was no magazine on the entire newsstand rack that had her in it. The ones that said they did didn't have good pictures.

Anyway, *People* had great titles, like "Mummy Dearest," where Anna could get the idea without having to read the article.

Stop it, she told herself. *I'd better stop paying too much attention or I'm going to get alienated all over again.*

Time to eat, but what?

She could go get a bowl of soup. She could afford it. But there's that problem of restaurants being depressing plus going out on the street when she knew it would smell of macaroni and cheese. No, no restaurant. It's just not worth the money except once in a while when she's ready to hang herself. No restaurant. Chris Evert. Chappaquiddick seemed like a diversion. More nostalgia.

Even the free handouts on the street had nothing to do with her life. She wasn't going to see Sister Rosa, faith healer. She didn't need artificial nails. Cheap therapy, now that might do some good. She didn't want a free Chicken McNugget with every three Big Macs. There was nothing left to do but go to sleep.

That night Anna had a strange dream. When the radiator knocked, she changed, but it wasn't waking. It was a half space filled with revelations. Each one about the dream. The dream.

Convinced, she fell back asleep. Compared with memory this was gentle and easy to slip into. But the second time the dream had more power. In it she was astonishingly vague. Trying to think at face value without realizing how much that was actually worth.

I could provide a description of giving head, she dreamed. *A head filled with breathtakingly beautiful images cannot pay attention to the radio or laundry, so bleed on me.*

She woke with the breath of a ghost on her back. She was green orange. Her orgasm was square. A pink star, a spider web, a dancing star too and a point and a shadow. A sky below, a calico rose in the middle of her skull. A red mask. A red egg. A moonscape made of glass. Magnified tongue cells. Salted spongy things. Mountains of black. Gray hills.

Chapter Three

As the sun came up Doc heard a little rustling from the kitchen. At first he assumed it was another family of mice to be hunted out and slaughtered. He resolved to set some little wooden traps and bait them with bits of rock-hard stale corn muffin. If the mice did not bite, the glue traps were next. Those wooden ones snapped their necks causing instant death without awareness. But the glue, though more efficient, caught frightened vermin squeaking away for help. Doc would throw them out the window hoping for total destruction on impact.

He heard the rustling again and then a thin whistle of wind, like some papers sailing onto his wooden kitchen floor. Further inspection revealed that some stranger, some unidentified person, had slipped a small pile of pages right under his door.

Attached to the first page was a short note.

> Dear Doctor,
> I received your business card on St. Mark's Place. We seem to have a common sensibility and I wonder if you might be the therapist for me. I am enclosing a term paper that I wrote for a college class thirteen years ago. Many of the same issues still plague me and I wanted you to see them in the intellectual and emotional context in which I experience them today. If you think that this is a case that interests you, please leave your door slightly ajar tomorrow at two o'clock.

Sincerely Yours,
Anna O.

Doc lay down on his couch, not even bothering to get dressed. He stretched out with two pillows and began to read.

ASSIGNMENT: Interpret your own dream using Freudian dream analysis.

Anna O.
Winter 1978
Freshman Seminar
Self, Culture, and Society
Professor Bertram Cohler

"'TIS THE STUFF THAT DREAMS ARE MADE OF"
A QUEST FOR IDENTITY THROUGH FREUDIAN DREAM ANALYSIS
by Anna O.

Freud claims that a dream is a symptom of a pathological idea. The dream is the "fulfillment of a wish" that is socially unacceptable.

THE DREAM

I was standing by the lake with Eleanor. I was shy and strong and in awe of her. We wore identical black tank suits and our bodies were changed to resemble each other. I was thinner and shorter with smaller breasts and hips. My hair was longer and fuller than usual.

She communicated to me, without gestures or noise, to dive into the lake. When I did, I discovered that I could breathe underwater. Then we were standing on the rocks by the shore, my hair was dry. She put her right arm around my waist in an authoritative man-

> ner, not an affectionate one, and guided me across the rocks.
>
> We walked over a coarse area without difficulty although there should have been some. She had me sit beside her on the rocks with our feet in the water. We watched the red sunset together.

In my dream, the most outstanding element was Eleanor and her power over me.

There were some inconsistencies in Eleanor.

1) She was physically altered.

2) She had superhuman abilities.

3) She enabled me to breathe underwater and walk over rocks without effort.

This makes me think that she represented more than herself. I think she represented a group of people with whom I share physical similarities. I assume that to be woman-kind in general.

We see that what appeared in the dream as Eleanor was actually what Freud calls a Composite Figure upon which numerous trains of thought converge.

> If the objects which are to be condensed into a single unity are much too incongruous, the dream work is often content with creating a composite structure with a comparatively distinct nucleus, accompanied by a number of less distinct features. (*The Interpretation of Dreams* p. 359)

In my dream, the unacceptable Dream Wish, which pertained to my relationships with women, was recast into a situation full of sensual and powerful symbols.

Freud also notes that dreams are sometimes composed of two different fantasies that coincide with each other at a few points. One of these points is superficial while the other is an interpretation of the first.

In my dream the superficial fantasy was being able to do what Eleanor could do. The underlying was finding solace in sexual relationships with women. It should be noted that a possible reason for such an ambiguous image as a setting sun might be because the thoughts at the base of this dream do not admit to visual representation.

The most important meaning for me, in the dream, is that after accepting these feelings and succumbing to Eleanor's power, my travels became effortless. In other words, my life became easier.

Even though I am only nineteen, I have seriously wondered if I could ever accept sexual feelings toward women without first making myself more feminine. This comes from a terror of masculinizing myself. Even though I know that women are better for me, I fear being told that I really want to be a man. It's an accusation that everyone seems to make.

So, if others thought I was more feminine than I currently am, they would stop accusing me of wanting to be a man. Then, I could have women's love more easily because I would not have to endure these kinds of assumptions. The fact that I had longer hair in the dream than I really do, confirms that I looked more feminine and therefore was able to relax and relate to Eleanor on a sexual level. But throughout all of these considerations, it is still the case that in no matter how many moments I may have wanted to conform to the social patterns of mainstream America, I have actually done nothing that would divert me from my present course of pursuit.

In conclusion, by using the psychoanalytic approach, it has been demonstrated how an unacceptable wish that was formed in the primary agency of the psyche was distorted by the secondary agency so that it could be rendered acceptable to consciousness. The second agency imposes cultural considerations upon a person's essentially a-cultural thought thereby showing that the particular person is also a social being, a product of culture.

END

A-
A thoughtful analysis of the dream that uses the power of Freud's technique in the best way. By the way, what happened to the concept of *representability* in the dream?
– B. Cohler

Chapter Four

By one-thirty the next afternoon, Doc was a nervous wreck. He paced and paced, opening and closing the refrigerator, rearranging all the food. Finally, at three minutes to the hour, he recovered somewhat and managed to slip delicately back into the office mentality.

Doc didn't believe in regular appointments. His patients only came when something was up. And even though Ms. O. didn't officially know the rules, something appeared to be definitely up. He hoped this would be more meaningful than most patient encounters. He hoped Anna O. would want to really discuss. Usually Doc just sat there while they talked about the unpleasant side of life. Then he did his bit.

Finally, at exactly two o'clock, he heard his door creak open and Doc saw a young woman standing in the threshold. She reminded him immediately of himself as a girl. She was a little pudgy, a little too soft. She had messy, romantic brown hair and noticed everything at once. She stepped into the room the same way he did, with a hesitant self-confidence. She had that kind of alienation that Doc recognized from years of therapy – somewhere between feeling exceptional and feeling like a clown. Anna came from the same kind of middle class that Doc knew oh-so-well. The kind that could pass up just as easily as down.

"Could I have something to drink?" she asked.

"Uhh." Doc walked over to the refrigerator. "I've got mayonnaise, cocktail sauce, Canada Dry, white rice, Hershey's chocolate milk, and boxed corn muffins."

"Water will be fine," she said. "I'll get it," following Doc into the dark kitchen.

"There's no electricity in the bathroom, bedroom, or kitchen," he said apologetically. "The whole place functions on extension cords."

Then he laughed the way a man is supposed to laugh when brushing off his own inadequacy.

"I love this neighborhood," she said.

"Yes," he answered. "Do you live here too?"

"Oh yes," she said. "I fit in perfectly. Everyone here has a secret and people they can't run into plus others they're always looking for. The potatoes are soft here. The wine is bad. It's strange here. Many people have died and left a lot of stuff for the living to avoid. There is baggage."

"Oh, your friends died of AIDS too," he said.

"Yes," she said. "And two got shot."

Anna settled into his couch and took a look around. The whole place was plain. There was no television, no tape player, no CD player, no VCR, no computer, no camera, no stereo. It was basic.

"You're a yes-and-no person, aren't you, Doc?" she asked.

"Yes," he said. "I believe in good and evil."

Anna looked him over, clumsily adjusting her skirt. Clumsily she crossed and uncrossed her legs.

"I find these clothes so humiliating," she said. "These stockings are so expensive. Your toenail becomes your worst enemy. Your couch is old-fashioned. I like that."

Doc smiled. He was still anxious about having admitted his belief system, so this slight compliment was warmly welcomed.

"I never buy anything interesting new," he said. "Just a coffeepot and towels."

They looked so much alike. Doc noticed that there was practically no difference except that Anna had to wear clothes that she hated and he could wear whatever he liked.

"I also believe in good and evil," Anna said. "Things are falling apart in this country with great rapidity and everyone wants to pretend that they have nothing to do with it. That no one is responsible. Now, I happen to be a happy person, Doc. I like *my* life the way it is. But when I look around for one minute I get … ideas. Ideas about structures."

"You mean politics?" he asked wistfully.

"Well, I do know that there are other things going on out there besides *my* happiness, if that's what you mean by politics."

"How strange," Doc mumbled and covertly made a note.

"What is it, Doc?" she asked, sinking back even more into the sofa's springless cushions, legs crossed tightly at the ankles. "What's wrong with me?"

"You're suffering from *empathy*," he said. "You must have some unresolved past experience."

"I have to go retouch my makeup now," she said. "I feel naked without it."

Waiting in his chair for Anna's return, Doc gleefully reserved judgment. He was so happy to find a patient with an intact set of beliefs. What a relief. Doc had had his since childhood and found it easier to get along with others who had their own beliefs too. When he was a kid, there were two systems. They were called Capitalism and Communism. Morality was easy then. Even later when he started thinking for himself, Doc could still tell right from wrong because both systems were wrong and the third system, the Imagination, was right. But these days there were no more easy Cold War systems to position himself against. Doc found this very trying personally because there was no longer an existing method for evaluating situations. Banality was the new enemy within.

Outside, global relations seemed to be one big blob. A comet. Out of control. One day Doc even crossed his fingers hoping that President Bush would die of a heart attack soon because nothing else he could imagine would get rid of that guy. It was a humiliating last resort, but he had to try everything.

Anna returned from the dark bathroom where she'd clearly thought things over.

"Well?" he asked gently.

"Well," she said, courageously. "I guess it all started with my childhood."

"I thought so," Doc said.

Then he waited. There is a way that people tell their secrets. If they make it into a big production, it's no secret. Only shame is the true indication of authentic camouflage.

Chapter Five

Anna sat back on the couch. She looked at Doc and then looked down at herself. She was relieved to have taken this step. Maybe things would be more soothing from now on. As Anna began to recite her autobiography, she felt even more comfortable. After all, she had long been the kind of person who explains herself regularly. It was part of a longstanding faith in being understood and a desire to apologize for every inadequacy. To ask forgiveness.

"Well ... let's see," she said, "should we start with school?"

"Sure."

"Well, elementary school was fine, I guess, until I started to get my own values. I remember exactly when that happened. It was one winter day, in class, when the teacher told us that light was the opposite of dark. I listened closely and tried to go along with it for some time. But then, that very evening, I noticed that light was *like* dark. Both were complete and ethereal, easily recognizable and metaphoric. That was when my problems began."

"Go on," Doc said.

"The next morning, on the subway to first grade, I decided to ask the teacher a question about the way that thoughts were structured – both his and mine. I wondered if everything was already known and each person just selected the facts that work for them. Or, were there still completely undetected ways to live?"

"What did he say?"

"My teacher couldn't cope. He seemed to be demanding over and over again that I justify my opinion. I couldn't just have it. That day, after nap time I walked into the wrong bathroom by mistake, and then made deals with God to get me out of that dump. Being doubted was so humiliating. I felt uncomfortable for the next twelve years."

Anna looked at Doc. He too was overweight. On a woman the fat goes right to her ego. Then every man on the street has to mention it for the rest of her life. Doc just had a potbelly, she noted. Surely no one ever said a thing about it.

"How is this revealed in your contemporary life?" Doc asked.

"Well, Doctor," she said, finally hooking her stockings on the jagged frame of the couch. "Doctor, in all my years of homosexuality I have never had sex with another lesbian. I've only made love to so-called straights or ambivalent bisexuals. Do you think that could be connected to not having been acknowledged as an intellectual?"

"Do most gay women love each other?" Doc asked.

"A lot of them love closeted movie stars," Anna answered thoughtfully. "But I can honestly say that most of them love each other too. They have more trouble with themselves."

"Anna," Doc said. "What were some of the explanations that have gone through your mind, historically, when you have faced this question?"

She tried hard to remember.

"Let's see. Well, I didn't like being told what to do. I didn't like being told that lesbians were the only group I could pick from."

"What else?"

"I'm in competition with men, clearly," Anna said. "Why should they be able to just walk in and have something that I can't have?"

"And what's that?" he asked.

"Straight women, of course."

"Well, that does sound logical," he said. "But it is also way off. What else?"

"Well, there's also that big lie about homosexuality. I don't believe that it's just this tiny little band of deviants. I've been crossing the thin line all my life on a regular basis. If they'll sleep with me, how straight can they be?"

"What else?"

"If a straight woman falls in love with me, she must really love me. If a gay woman loves me, she's just a lesbian looking for a girlfriend."

"You do amazing things with logic," Doc said, writing furiously. "What else?"

"Well, men who are much less than I am get a lot of breaks. They're judged differently. I wanted to be judged like they are judged."

"What else?"

"It's hard to love a beggar."

"Do you prefer pornography or sex?" Doc asked.

"Sex," Anna said.

"Anything else?" Doc asked.

"Yes," she said. "On top of all my personal problems there are these social problems. There are these facts about my friends dying of AIDS. I'm thirty-one years old, Doctor, and I read the obituary page first."

"I think we need to start at the beginning," Doc said. "Let us start with your family. How do you feel about your family?"

Anna crossed her legs and arms in an unconscious attempt to protect her genitals.

"My family seems so unreal to me. And when I am with them, I also am not real. I am a character in some movie and someone else wrote the script. Doc, did you ever read Delmore Schwartz's *In Dreams Begin Responsibilities*? In the opening piece a man walks into a movie theater, and there on the screen is the story of his parents' lives. The story of how they met. He watches, amazed as he sees his parents' courtship projected before him. They walk along the Coney Island boardwalk. They're young, in love. Finally, Schwartz can't take it anymore. He leaps up from his seat in the dark and yells, 'Don't do it. It's not too late to change your minds. Nothing good will come of it, only remorse, hatred, scandal, and two children whose characters are monstrous.'"

"Now, Anna, I know that patients often reveal unconscious wishes in seemingly casual anecdotes. So tell me, if you imagined that your family was a movie, what would it look like? What would happen on the screen?"

"Well, Doc," she said, "it would go something like this."

Chapter Six

FADE IN

EXT. NEW YORK CITY STREET. EARLY SUNDAY MORNING 1990.

The streets are empty but covered by the garbage left over from Saturday night. ANNA, *a thirty-year-old woman, is crossing the street toward the subway entrance. She is dressed up awkwardly, so that she stumbles slightly in high heels.*
She passes a MAN *leaning against the subway entrance smoking from a crack pipe.*

MAN

I want to lick your pussy.

ANNA

I'm going to a funeral.

MAN

I hope it's not someone close.

INT. HALLWAY OF AN OLD-FASHIONED APARTMENT BUILDING.

ANNA *rings the bell. Her mother,* RUTH, *opens the door.* RUTH *is simply but appropriately dressed. She does not dye her hair and she wears no makeup beyond a little lipstick.*

RUTH

Thank God you wore a dress.

ANNA

Hi, Ma.

RUTH

But your hair is too short.

INT. RUTH AND IRV'S APARTMENT. MODESTLY DECORATED AND COMFORTABLE BUT FINANCIALLY SECURE.

ANNA

Where's Pop?

RUTH

He went to rent a car.

INT. RUTH AND IRV'S LIVING ROOM. PHOTOS AND OTHER MEMORABILIA ON THE MANTELPIECE. BOOKS VISIBLE ON THE SHELVES INCLUDE *PORTNOY'S COMPLAINT*, ISAAC SINGER, AND TWO ROWS OF BOOKS BY FREUD.

STEVE, *Anna's brother, enters the room. Although he is two years younger, he is much more comfortable in his funereal garb. Yet he is generally uncomfortable personally.*

STEVE

Hi, Anna.

They kiss.

STEVE

I flew in as soon as my secretary gave me the message.

ANNA

Where's Pop?

STEVE

He went to rent a car.

BARBARA, *their younger sister, enters the room. She is twenty and, in addition to being chronologically younger, she also plays the role of the baby of the family.*

ANNA

Hi, Barb.

BARB

Hi, Anna. Pop went to get a car.

STEVE

Barb, your shoes aren't shined.

ANNA

Steve, give her a break. She's old enough to dress herself.

STEVE

Then why doesn't she?

BARB

Mom's been trashing Morris all morning. I think she feels guilty that he croaked.

RUTH

Guilty? I don't have anything to feel guilty about. The man was a fascist pure and simple. I know he was your father's childhood friend, but he was a Republican. He was against busing but for the wrong reasons.

ANNA

Where's Pop? It's almost two hours to the cemetery.

RUTH

He had to take care of a patient who is suicidal and then he had to rent a car.

ANNA

A what?

STEVE, BARB, RUTH

A car!

INT. A RENTED CAR. ONE HOUR LATER. DRIVING TO LONG ISLAND.

IRV *is driving.* RUTH *is sitting next to him. The three children are in the backseat.*

RUTH

He was a real Republican. He voted for Goldwater. I remember I told him I voted for Henry Wallace and he said, "Who?" Whenever a black person came into his travel agency he would follow them around to make sure they didn't steal anything.

BARB

What can you steal in a travel agency?

STEVE

Mom, you should see what it's like living in the South. If you pull over at one of those rest stops on the highway, they sell little salt and pepper shakers of black mammies eating watermelon.

ANNA

What do your students say about it?

STEVE

They don't notice. The university is all white so the students' lives are all white. Black people are something they see on television or public transportation.

IRV

I don't get it. I just don't get it.

BARB

What don't you get, Pop?

IRV

He was sitting in a chair and then he slumped over, dead. Was it cardiovascular arrest or an aneurism? I don't know.

INT. THE CAR DRIVES UP TO THE FUNERAL CHAPEL IN SUBURBAN LONG ISLAND.

RUTH

Here we are.

STEVE

Where do we park?

BARB

Pop, pull into the shopping mall across the street.

RUTH

Irv, park in the mall.

IRV

Where should I park?

RUTH

In the mall.

ANNA

There's Sylvia.

RUTH

There's Morris's sister.

IRV

She's the oldest and she had to watch her younger brother die.

BARB

I hope I die first.

RUTH

Her husband died. Her daughter's in the Peace Corps.

EXT. IN FRONT OF THE FUNERAL HOME.

SYLVIA, *very distraught, is standing in front of the funeral home.* ANNA *is the first to reach her as the others walk over, one by one, from the parking lot.*

ANNA

Sylvia.

SYLVIA

I don't know how I feel. I don't know how I feel. I'm not feeling anything. I can't cry. I just can't cry.

STEVE

Sylvia, how are you doing?

SYLVIA

I don't know. I don't know. I can't cry. I'm not able to cry. I don't know how I feel. I don't know.

BARB

Hi, Sylvia.

SYLVIA

I was just telling your sister and your brother how I don't know what I feel. I'm not feeling a thing. I was just telling them. Not a thing.

RUTH

Sylvia.

SYLVIA

Ruthie. I was just telling the kids that I haven't been able to cry. Not a tear. Where's Irv?

RUTH

He's parking the car.

SYLVIA

Look at you, you're all so broken up. Me? I don't know what I feel.

INT. THE LOBBY OF THE FUNERAL HOME.

The three siblings are standing together awkwardly, surrounded by short relatives.

HILDA FRIEDMAN

You don't remember me but I'm your daddy's second cousin, Hilda Friedman. This is my husband, Izzy, and that's my sister Frieda Shluvsky. You're such a big girl now, how old are you?

ANNA

Thirty.

SOPHIE PEARLMAN

Remember me? I'm your cousin Sophie Pearlman from Glendale. I remember Stevie when you were just a little boy. You came to my store in the Bronx and you wet your pants, wee-wee all over the floor. What are you doing now?

STEVE

I teach semiotics.

SOPHIE

And you, you're still the baby.

BARB

Yeah.

IRV *enters the room.*

HILDA

There's your father. Irv, can you believe it?

IRV

Hilda, how are you?

HILDA

Eh, the diabetes. You shouldn't know.

IRV

Are you taking medication?

HILDA

Yeah, but the real problem is Izzy.
(*Loud voice.*)
Izzy, wake up, it's Irv, the doctor. Irv, Izzy had a psychotic break.

IRV

No kidding?

IZZY

Could you believe it?

IRV

How are you feeling?

IZZY

Not too good.

SYLVIA *enters.*

SYLVIA

Irv, I've been looking all over for you. I'm all alone here.

IRV

How are you doing, Sylvia?

SYLVIA

I can't cry. I just can't cry.

INT. THE WAITING ROOM OF THE FUNERAL HOME. PEOPLE ARE LOOKING AT THEIR WATCHES.

IRV *is talking to two old men in polyester suits and yarmulkes.*

JOEY WARSHOFSKY

So, Irv, then she had the radium implants.

IRV

That must have been difficult for you.

STEVE

How are you doing, Pop?

IRV

Steve, you know the Warshofsky boys, Yankel and Joey.

STEVE

How are you?

YANKEL

Not so good.

STEVE *is obviously embarrassed by the whole scene. He doesn't want to have anything to do with these people and can't understand why his father is so connected to them.*

IRV

Stevie, Yankel was just telling me about some illness in his family.

YANKEL

Yeah, Irv, it's the circulation. Look, my leg, it only goes this far.

STEVE

Dad, we've got to go into the chapel now.

IRV

One minute.

JOEY

I tell ya, Irv, it was a big shock to have Morris go so quickly.

IRV

I am shocked.

JOEY

That guy was built like a horse. He took his pressure five times a day. He never touched a piece of meat. A real vegetarian.

YANKEL

I could have sworn you'd go first, Irv. What with your lousy history and all. To tell you the truth, this is quite a shock.

IRV

I am shocked.

INT. IN THE CHAPEL.

All the mourners are seated in pews. RUTH, IRV, *and* SYLVIA *are on one side of the first row.* ANNA, STEVE, *and* BARB *are sitting together in the back.*

BARB

Who are all these people? I can't believe I'm related to them. Who's that?

ANNA

That's Shirley Weintraub. She married a Christian and her father never spoke to her again.

BARB

Which one is her father?

ANNA

Walter, the dissipated one in the third row.

BARB

What a jerk. What is he, religious?

ANNA

No, he's a shmuck.

STEVE

Now Morris is dead and Shirley and Walter are in the same room for the first time in ten years.

RABBI

Morris Levine had a life. He was born in the Bronx in 1923. He worked hard for his parents in their small shoe repair shop. He was a perfect son. When his country called him to duty he fought bravely at D Day. And true to his sense of responsibility Morris returned to the shop. Twenty-five years later when his father died, Morris took over the shop and turned it into a thriving travel agency. Years from now when we think of Morris we'll say, "Morris, thanks for the memories." Morris Levine will be laid to his eternal rest at Beth Sefer Torah, on exit fourteen.

EXT. OUTSIDE THE CHAPEL AS THE MOURNERS ARE FILING OUT. LATE AFTERNOON

RUTH

Look at Walter. He looks awful. He should, the way he treated his own daughter.

IRV

What can you do?

RUTH

Who, Walter?

IRV

No, Morris. He just fell over and he was dead. He didn't even know it was happening.

WALTER *comes running over.*

WALTER

Irv, Irv, come quick. It's Sophie Pearlman. She passed out.

RUTH

Don't tell me.

IRV

I'm coming.

ANNA

Dad, you're running around taking care of everybody and no one is taking care of you.

IRV

That's what happens when you're a doctor – you get used to it.

INT. MORRIS'S SMALL BRONX APARTMENT.

At the shiva. Lots of close-ups of the deli platters. The relatives are gobbling smoked meat.

JOEY WARSHOFSKY

Good tongue. The best.

AUNT MOLLY

Anna, do you remember me? I'm your Aunt Molly from Chicago.

ANNA

How are you, Molly? How are your children?

MOLLY

Good. My daughter, Sheila, she married a rabbi. They've got two healthy girls. But my oldest son, Leon, isn't doing too good.

ANNA

What's the matter?

MOLLY

Well, he's forty years old. He's still single and he lives all alone in Key West.

INT. ONE CORNER OF THE LIVING ROOM AT MORRIS'S APARTMENT.

IRV *is sitting alone looking through a stack of books.*

BARB

What are you looking at, Pop?

IRV

These books Morris was reading. He must have five hundred dollars worth of books here.

BARB

What kind of books?

IRV

How to Avoid Stress, Eat Right to Live Long, Living without Stress, Better Diet for a Stress-Free Life. What was he so anxious about? I feel like I didn't even know him.

INT. ANOTHER CORNER OF THE LIVING ROOM IN MORRIS'S APARTMENT.

ANNA *is sitting on a couch talking to an eighty-five-year-old Orthodox Jew with a beard and hat.*

ANNA

So, Uncle Fischl, what's new?

FISCHL

Listen. When my father died, I went every day to the cemetery. And every night he would come to haunt me in my dreams. The next day I would go to the cemetery and plead with him to leave me alone, leave me alone. But every night he would come back again to haunt me. Finally, I couldn't take it anymore. I went to the rabbi. I said, "Rabbi, every night my father comes to me in my dreams and every day I go to the cemetery and beg him to stay away. But he won't listen. What should I do?" Do you know what the rabbi said?

ANNA

What?

FISCHL

He said, "Stop going to the cemetery."

INT. THE KITCHEN.

STEVE *goes over to* SYLVIA *sitting alone in a chair.*

STEVE

Sylvia, do you want me to make you a sandwich?

SYLVIA

I'm sick to my stomach. I couldn't eat a thing.

STEVE

Do you want me to bring you some ginger ale?

SYLVIA

I'm telling you, I'm so mad at that guy.

STEVE

At who?

SYLVIA

At that stinking brother of mine.

STEVE

Because he died?

SYLVIA

Because he died.

EXT. IN FRONT OF MORRIS'S BUILDING.

IRV *and* WALTER *are standing together outside the house.* ANNA *stands next to her father holding his coat.*

IRV

I'm going back to Manhattan now, Walter, but I just want to know how you're feeling.

WALTER

I'm angry, Irv.

IRV

What are you angry at?

WALTER

I'm angry at you, Irv. You don't give a shit about me or any of your old friends. You left the Bronx and became a big-shot psychiatrist. I know you look down on all of us. You never call to ask how I'm doing. Then you call me out of the blue to say that Morris is dead. You wanna know why you're such an asshole, Irv?

IRV

Why?

WALTER

Because you're a snob and a phony. You're a phony, Irv. You don't give a shit about any of us and you didn't give a shit about Morris.

IRV

Walter, I know you're angry at me, and I know you think I've done some bad things and I probably have. But I also think you're angry about something else.

WALTER

You're right, Irv. I'm angry at myself.

IRV

Look, anytime you want to come to my office and talk, just give me a call. I always have time for you.

EXT. THE STREET IN FRONT OF MORRIS'S BUILDING.

ANNA *and* IRV *are walking down the block to the car where the rest of the family is waiting.*

ANNA

Pop, why did you let Walter yell at you like that? This is your friend's funeral. People should be nice to you.

IRV

So, I helped him out a little bit. He can't hurt me. He doesn't even know who he is.

INT. IN THE CAR GOING BACK TO MANHATTAN. SUNSET ON THE BRIDGE.

ANNA

Hey, Ma. You never told me that cousin Leon is gay.

RUTH

He's not gay. He's lonely.

ANNA

Oh, come on. Get over it, Ma. You think in the whole family I'm the only one?

IRV

Anna is right, Ruth. Plenty of lonely people are gay.

ANNA

That's not what I said. Stevie, tell them.

STEVE

Don't drag me into it.

ANNA

This is so predictable.

RUTH

Did you see that expression on Hilda Friedman's face? I thought she was going to jump into the grave right after him.

IRV

She was always in love with Morris. For thirty years they used to go out for breakfast together once a month. Even last Wednesday they went.

STEVE

You two are always thinking about what other people are feeling. I just found out in therapy that most families don't talk like this.

IRV

All Jewish families talk like this.

STEVE

No they don't. Do you think the people in the other cars are saying, "Poor Irv, this must be so hard for him?" No, they're saying, "Did you see that dress she wore?"

IRV

(*Very angry. Suddenly out of control.*)

No they're not. They're all concerned. They're all concerned about how the other one feels.

BARB

Pop, be careful, you'll have a heart attack.

IRV

What are you talking about? Don't tell me not to die. You don't die. You don't die.

BARB

It's a deal.

IRV

This is no time for jokes.

END

Chapter Seven

When Anna went home at the end of the session, Doc took out his old manual typewriter and began to write up the case. Obviously she was angry at her family. But she tried to avoid it by being superior, by being detached from their prejudice. It all broke down, though, in the last scene in the car where Anna made herself vulnerable to her mother's homophobia for the millionth time. That's when she finally felt intimate.

Doc was more interested in Anna's experiences as a young intellectual. At the age of six her mode of inquiry had already been rejected. Doc's own experience had been quite the opposite. Especially in high school, when he suddenly became quite grandiose and unleashed some kind of attractive power. The other kids gave him their attention, demanding engagement on a wide range of passionate questions. They demanded that he tell them exactly how the world should go. Then they would argue with him forever about the details. The whole conversation was worth it from the beginning to end because it was their world at stake. After all they would eventually run it. Then the change came. Some guys chose hockey sticks but Doc chose Goodwill. He said it was a process.

To this day Doc held those beliefs. His goal was about *how* we get there because, after all, we might never arrive. So, what he did on the way might later turn out to have been the entirety of his life. People were innately entitled, Doc believed, to more options than crossing their fingers or standing in line to buy lottery tickets. But Goodwill was fairly vague as far as destinations go. How could he try for it? How could he stop?

Phew, Doc said. *This stuff is like an old friend on a new street.*

Then he lay down on the couch.

On one hand Doc was still dreaming of a better world. However, he also feared that a degree of callousness was required to see possibilities as everything falls apart. He feared this was a quality he might hold. He recalled from his childhood that this kind of thinking can lead to moving sidewalks and other white chrome solutions, all of which require advertising. Doc feared he might wake up one morning with an idea like Muzak. He might have really bad ideas just like those people who say, "There are too many criminals so let's build malls to contain the shoppers."

Even when Doc relaxed and could see people very clearly, he could not avoid their speed and panic. In fact, it gave him a few minutes of his own panic.

I'm panicking, he thought.

Later he looked in the mirror and remembered he had a face like Lenny Bruce. Thank God, not pretentious but don't get drunk together or it'll be rape.

"It's okay, I'm only panicking," he said, lying down. Then he crossed his hands on his chest and looked at the wall.

All night the doctor lay there, listening to the muffled snap of mousetraps echoing in the alley. He was tossing and turning, thinking about his own childhood. His own set of parents.

When Doc was a kid the house was crazy. There were always people staying there. When Grandpa died, Grandma came to live with them because he'd only left enough money to pay for the funeral. There was nothing left for her. Later this guy named Napping Sam Glukowsky came. He taught little Doc how to play chess. When Sam was lonely, and couldn't sleep anymore, he'd take Doc to the park to play chess with the other men. After him a guy named Jakey Levine came. He was a professor. His wife threw him out because he was acting crazy so he came to live with Doc instead. Pop said Jake was just depressed but grandma used to say, "Jake's got a *loch in kopf*."

Well, she was the only one who knew because, as it turned out, he wasn't crazy but he had a brain tumor. Only nobody knew that yet.

Jake was very confused. He forgot how people decided what to do all day so he used to go to the UN and sit there. He didn't know what else to do. Sometimes he would meet a strange woman and bring her back to the house. He wanted Grandma to cook her dinner. But, after talking to Jake for a few hours the woman would figure out that he didn't know what he was talking about, so she would leave.

He had these term papers that his students had written but he couldn't correct or grade them because he couldn't understand them. One night when Doc's parents were out and his sister and baby brother were asleep, Doc and Grandma and Jake sat on the couch trying to figure out what to do with the papers. Finally Jake got some clarity. He took those wooden building blocks that the kids played with and made boxes on the floor. One was A, one was B, one was C, and one was Fail. The doc and Grandma threw the papers and whatever they landed in, that was their grade.

Doc tried to play chess, but as soon as Jake was losing he would say "Oops" and turn over the board.

He also was filthy. He never took a bath. He slept in his clothes and smoked cigarettes. He slept on the couch in the living room in his black trench coat that he never took off. Doc gave him a present for Hanukkah. It was a bar of soap.

Once Jake's daughter came from New Jersey to visit him. Doc was about eight and she was about seven or eight. The three of them were sitting on the couch and Jake was saying something but he didn't know what he was talking about. He forgot what words meant and didn't know how to explain anything. Later his daughter said to Doc, "When I grow up I want to be a lesbian." It was the first time he'd ever heard that word.

Jake died.

A lot of things happen when you're eight, he thought. *And a lot of it is very important information. If you listen closely when people talk and look at the expressions on their faces, you will never forget them. Even when they die or disappear, you will always know how they felt and later, if you ever have that feeling, you will remember what it looked like on another person's face. If you listen you won't lose it. You will remember.*

That's what it was like to live in that family. There were always people standing in front of you being vulnerable. Doc had a cousin named Shmul Rabinowitz. He was Orthodox, from Brooklyn. He was maybe twenty-three. Doc was nine. Shmul would come over to the apartment with an orange, a paper plate, and plastic knife because nothing there was kosher. One night Doc's mom and pop were at the movies. His grandmother was in Miami. Then Shmul came over. He used to come over when he was upset and talk to Pop, but Pop wasn't there so he talked to Doc.

Doc sat and listened for almost three hours. His feet didn't even touch the ground. Shmul went on and on. He talked very quickly in that Old World style, and he talked about God and what happens after you die and what hell is like. The whole time Doc sat, listening and making it possible for Shmul to talk. It was his first experience in psychoanalysis.

When Shmul left the house he went to the top of Mount Sinai Hospital and jumped off. Later they had to pretend he was hit by a car so he could be buried in a Jewish cemetery. Everyone walked around talking about "the accident."

How did I know what to do? Doc wondered. *I was just a little kid.*

All his life Doc watched his parents calmly listen to people who were out of control. A lot of people would come over when they were very upset. One woman had a son who died of meningitis. Doc also had meningitis. But he lived and the other boy died. That woman got drunk and came over and was screaming at Doc's mom that her son had died while Doc had lived. Later, that woman used to have fights with her husband and come over to use the phone and yell at him. While she screamed, Mom sat at the kitchen table with a cup of coffee. That was how Doc was taught such a high level of tolerance for maniacal behavior. It was some sense of professional obligation without the benefit of office hours. Doc's parents couldn't draw the line. They were listeners and afterward they would discuss. Many Jewish people grew up in homes with yelling. Doc's family had yelling but they weren't the ones doing it. They were sitting, listening, and the yellers came to them.

Chapter Eight

Oh, for the good old days of 1980, Doc thought. *There was so much great stuff in the mirror then. All those horrible painful disasters that I did not see and had never heard of little more than a decade ago. Now they're everyday life.*

The worst problem, back then, was that if people did not do something dramatic, immediately, the future would be awful. But they didn't do it. Doc experienced this lack of action as a terrible personal embarrassment. It just reminded him, once again, of his and all human inadequacies.

Now he couldn't face himself because he didn't know how to act. And spirituality wasn't going to do it this time. The only leftover from Jewish theology in this doctor's life was an aversion to Jesus Christ. He had no other religion. Not even the Shirelles.

Then it was time for his next patient, the Complainer.

"Mexico was too hot," he said. "The people weren't fun. I'm tired of being poverty-stricken. I need money to buy new furniture for my apartment."

"How did you get your apartment?" Doc asked, knowing it was his responsibility to pose probing questions.

"My parents paid for it. I had to do all the organizing. I had to work and work. I had to supervise the people who did the labor. It was terrible. I was a victim. My parents paid for it, but I deserved it."

The Complainer was utterly lifeless. He was the bland kind of guy they used to show on Alka-Seltzer commercials. His lips were scrunched into a permanent sneer of distaste while his eyes looked puppy-dog-like and begged for sympathy. He wasn't what you'd call a good time.

"Who pays your dental bills?" Doc asked.

"My parents do. They have to because I don't know how to work. I have no idea of what supporting myself really means. How am I supposed to get a job without experience? Especially in this economy?"

"You mean you've never worked?"

"Of course I've worked. But, I've never been paid for it. That's because an artist is the most undervalued person in this society. At least if I was black I could get a grant. But no one gives a shit about a white guy like me."

"Why not?"

"Doc, let me explain it to you. I am a victim. Get it, Doc? A victim."

The Complainer sat there. His name was John but Doc called him Cro-Mag because he was so unevolved.

"Do you know what poor means?" Doc asked.

"I am poor. I am poverty-stricken. I have nothing except for an eighty-thousand-dollar co-op. Do you know that means on today's market? It means nothing."

"Well, what would give your life more meaning?" Doc asked, quietly, repressing his own desire to strangle this guy.

"You know, I'd like to do something heroic, have an adventure. Like Francis Ford Coppola making *Apocalypse Now*. I'd like to take a few million, go down to some Third World country, hire a couple thousand natives at a dollar a day and really take a risk."

"What risk did Francis Ford Coppola take?"

"Doc, he mortgaged his house!"

"Well, John, you can have life-shattering experiences in your own neighborhood. You could ... well, you know ... you could do something for ... someone else."

"Politics is boring," Cro-Mag said in a drippy way. "It's hopeless. I wouldn't have any fun. Besides, I'm too poor. I don't have time to be political."

"There are people sleeping in the park in shelters made of plastic and cardboard," said Doc. "There are people living around the park in co-ops and condominiums like Christadora House and Eastbeth. The police tear down the tents of the homeless. Now, I'm going to ask you a trick question."

Doc was using cognitive therapy.

"Who are the victims?"

"I am," said Cro-Mag. "I am the biggest victim."

"What are you going to do tomorrow?" Doc asked.

"Tomorrow I will sleep till noon. Then I will go to a coffee shop and pay someone else to cook and serve me breakfast. Then I will go home and do errands and make notes. Then I will make phone calls. Then I will do something else. Then I will go to the gym. Then I will eat dinner in a restaurant. Then I will go to an art event. Then I will go to a bar or watch TV and get drunk or maybe I will find a twenty-one-year-old who will feel sorry for me and have sex with me. Then I will go to sleep."

"And if you were not a victim, then what?"

"If was not a victim I would wake up around noon and have sex with someone who did not have a job to go to either. Then she and I would talk about what geniuses we are. Then I would get a phone call from a fancy museum and mail from a foundation. Then my girlfriend would do the vegetable shopping. Then I would go to the gym. Then she would tell me that I am brilliant. That I am a great artist."

"How are you going to get from here to there?" Doc asked.

"I don't know," Cro-Mag said.

"I can see why," Doc said.

Later Doc placed Cro-Mag squarely in relation to his other issues. Was mankind de-evolving? Survival of the least interesting?

Doc was willing to continue this study of the stupefaction of the privileged, but he had to be careful. Too much time with Cro-Mag was like watching television. Like holding a magnifying glass to a bottomless pit.

They became what they beheld, he remembered, and gave Blake the last word.

Chapter Nine

Frail state. Frightened star. Sensual feeling. Anna was doubly affected. Recognizing others' masturbatory habits, she too needed a feeling and not a thought. But that raised the question of *style* and what one was. It's a romance, that's for sure. Some mythical visceral experience or a box a person fits into for other purposes. Something to swear by, even more. She'd never thought about this before.

On the street there was a Hyundai seething with criticism. Then Anna digressed back to that desired state where *think* is a sequence toward a solution. It's all about logic. Anna stared ahead at the dirty city street. She had to concentrate really hard to think it through for herself. Something wasn't right. There was something not true about Doc. There was something a little off. Thank God for logical conclusions: they are an activity of pure permission.

She noticed a young homeless man doing the Sunday *Times Magazine* crossword puzzle. Anna couldn't know how badly he felt.

"Can't you say something nice?" the homeless man asked when he caught her staring.

"Undulating vulvas," Anna said. "Pistachio, sky blue, red-and-white stripes, bare blue ass kiss, guess who."

"Okay," the guy said. "Now back to the insults."

The next woman who passed wore eyeglass frames whose color reinforced the illusion that she was a redhead.

Maybe that explains the problem I've always had with female identification, she thought. *It's like looking at Picasso's* Three Women *only to come away thinking, "My breast is your thigh."*

These thoughts illuminated the weird formation that broke up Anna. The whole experience became some sort of bucolic mutilation as she climbed the stairs to therapy.

"So what brings you to therapy today?" Doc asked.

"Well, there are a number of things on my mind," Anna said. "I was sitting in NYU Medical Center, in the Co-Op Care, massaging the feet of another friend of mine who is dying, in this case named Paul. Then I realized that I have a lot of unresolved anger."

"Why do you massage the feet of dying people?"

"Well," Anna answered, "the reason we massage the feet of dying people is because they have been in bed for a long, long time and have poor circulation in their feet. They need to be touched but chest catheters and IVs get in the way. Besides, they can't sit up. By rubbing their feet, you sit on the edge of their beds and they can see you. You can talk to them and touch them at the same time without them having to move. You can take one long last look."

Silence.

"Here, Doc, I brought in some show-and-tell."

She handed him a folded-up newspaper clipping with circles drawn around different items. She held her breath, waiting to see his reaction, Doc read out loud.

WOMEN SEEKING WOMEN

MWF, 40, wants to fulfill fantasy for the first-time encounter with gay or Bi female. Must be discreet, Spfld. Area 4052.

MWBiF would like to meet M/SBiWF 18-30 for fun and friendship. Hart Area 10437.

MbiWF, 31, feminine, looking for feminine M/SbiWF for discreet intimate friendship. FF Area 30351.

MEN SEEKING MEN

> Bi/dude great videos, discreet fun. No gays! Macho Spanish dudes, straight-bi and closet "men in uniform" welcome. Absolute discretion. Mark Box 554, Newton CT. 06470.
>
> BiWM 29 6'2" very attractive muscular discreet seeking a muscular handsome straight-acting G/BiWM 22-32. NH area 50410.

"What is this?" Doc asked.

"It's an oppression document," Anna said. "File it under O."

"Not only are they all *discreet*," Doc said, looking it over, "but being white seems to take on paramount importance."

"I hope I live to see the day," Anna said, rearranging the cushions on the couch, "when the words *straight-acting* have naturally disappeared from the English language. And Doc, don't you dare tell me that *all people are basically bisexual*. I don't think I could take it."

"Why not?"

"Well, you know," she said, "when I was a teenager the rule was that everyone was really heterosexual and since I wasn't, I became really deviant. Now the rhetoric seems to be going in the direction of everyone being really bisexual and I'm not that either. So I'm still a deviant. Blame it on Freud, right?"

"Freud is only an idea. It can work for you or against you."

That was a good sign, Anna thought, deciding to take the next step.

"Do you do dream analysis, Doc? Is that where all this is leading? I mean I did have a strange one last night. It was a strange night."

Anna felt somewhat dowdy, not fitting properly into her dress.

"It was a strange night. It was gray and very cold. I was thinking about all the women I've ever loved. I was thinking about each one of them individually. The opera singer who couldn't stop coming and the waitress who didn't know how. I was thinking about the women who had to fight for their orgasms and the ones who got theirs like they got their lunch. I was lonely because of the weather. I was reviewing all the ways that my life has been propelled by strategizing for access to the female body."

"Did it feel good?"

"Well, Doc, each encounter left me with some erotic memory. You know, a flash of something she said. Some small gesture or the way she moved her body. Something that really pleased me. Then I fell asleep and had this dream."

"What did you dream?"

"I dreamt that I took William Burrough's penis and tied it up with piano wire. I hung him like a Chagall painting. He's an old feeble man so he swayed in the wind."

"Then what?"

"Then, in my dream, I took a rapist's penis and grafted it onto his forehead. He had to walk around all day with his own dick in his face. I called it *Surrealism*."

"How does the rapist fit into it?"

"Well, Doc," Anna answered, like she'd already thought this one through, "a lot of my lovers have been raped. Easily half. Some were raped twice. One was gang raped twice. And, well ... I began to wonder, recently, if I might have had something to do with it."

"With them being raped?"

"No, with them coming to me. I mean, I began to wonder if I was especially attractive to women who had been multiply violated. Women who were not safe."

"You mean," Doc said, with a twinkle in his eye, "you mean you worry that these women look to you for the father/protector they never had."

"What an odd comment," Anna said. "What a terrifying thought. What a confusing possibility. What a construction. My father takes care of people and I do too. Does that mean I have problems with my femininity? I mean, after all, Doc, the reason I've been involved with so many women who have been hurt might actually have something more to do with demographics and the gene pool. I mean, most women that I meet have fairly normal female experiences. And being raped seems to be ... well ... a natural part of all that. I don't mean *natural*, like destiny. But it is awfully common. It's not just me. So, now comes the interesting part of the dream."

"Oh goody," Doc said.

"In the next part J.G. Ballard swam through streets of female urine. The girls read his book *Crash* and then mowed him down with their Volkswagen, crushing his chest slowly against a brick wall. As he screamed in agony larger than representation can accommodate, they referred to his text and had orgasms. Later, they jumped up and down yelling, 'You're not a hero. You're not a hero. You're not. You're not. You're not.'"

"How do you analyze that part of the dream, Anna?"

She paused, suddenly shy.

"I guess I'm nervous about my birthday."

"Oh, come on. You can do better than that."

"Doc, it's just that we've ... we've ... we've been so oppressed."

"Anna, your dream seems to be about a justifiable revenge. The women in your life have been hurt by men. There's nothing wrong with wanting to protect them."

"But, Doctor, how can I protect them if I'm one of them?"

"Uh ..."

"Doctor, have you ever been in therapy yourself?"

"Nope."

"Figures."

"You know why?" he said, leaning over. "You tell them one real thing and then the doctor thinks he knows you. He starts getting arrogant and overfamiliar, making insulting suggestions left and right. You have to protest constantly just to set the record straight. Finally he makes offensive assumptions and throws them in your face. A stranger in a bar could do the same. You know what, Anna?"

"What, Doc?"

"I have secrets I'd like to tell. There are things I need to figure out, out loud. But I would only tell them to someone who would never need use it."

"Use it how?"

"To get ahead. To get revenge. To get better. To get started. You know, to win."

"Gee, Doc, someone must have really hurt your feelings."

"Yes," Doc said wearily. "I only want friends who never expect to *win*."

That's when she realized she missed that one friend. But she hid it behind incremental blocks of description.

Chapter Ten

Doc waited impatiently for Anna to return from the bathroom so that the session could resume.

"Doc," she said, crouched over, "there is something that has been particularly weighing on my mind. Something I want to resolve while I have the will and strength of character to face it."

"What?"

"Well, Doc ... I never had a lover who let me meet her parents."

"Why not?" he asked.

"Because sometimes they just couldn't. Sometimes they had no parents. Sometimes their parents were back home in some small town in Pennsylvania or the Bronx where these daughters just didn't make sense. But there were also times, Doc, when the women were ... ashamed of me. It was because they were ashamed of me. Because they thought I was less. Because they didn't want to make their families uncomfortable, so they made me uncomfortable instead."

"Are you sure?" Doc asked.

"I'm absolutely sure," she said.

"Give me an example," Doc said.

"Some girl named Sarah fell in love with me. We hitch-hiked across America, stopping off in Chicago where she fucked her ex-boyfriend. Three days later, in a parking lot by the Bonneville Salt Flats, she said, 'You think I'm a homosexual but I'm not.'"

Oh my God, Doc thought. *That's exactly what that woman in white leather said to me. Only why did she say that to me? I'm a man. I'm supposed to be immune to that sort of thing.*

"Then what happened?"

"We went to California anyway. I only had twenty-six dollars and couldn't very well turn around and hitch-hike back to New York alone. I could get raped. Spent a few weeks picking walnuts in her hometown of Visalia and ate potato dinners followed by harassing questions by her family."

"Hold everything, Anna," Doc said. "I though you said you never had a lover who let you meet her parents."

"We weren't lovers anymore, remember? She'd gone straight conveniently in Utah."

"Oh yeah."

"So, one day we're hanging out by the one and only hot dog stand on Visalia's main drag and her father reached into his car and handed me a present. 'Here's something you might be interested in,' he says. It was a book called *The History of Deviance in America*."

It seemed to Doc that her time was almost up, but he decided to make it a double session.

"So then, Doc, we go to LA where she picks up some guy on the UCLA campus and we end up living with him. Me, sleeping in the living room in a condo in Westwood, listening to them fucking. Finally, she realizes that she's pregnant from that guy in Chicago. I spent three days sitting silently beside her in welfare centers and abortion clinics until the Medi-Cal came through and she gets it paid for. See, I was still acting like a lover. So, the night after the operation we're eating in that guy's apartment and news comes on the TV that Medicaid abortions have just been outlawed by the Hyde amendment. The next morning I told that guy, 'Buy me a one-way to New York or I'll break your legs.'"

"Did he do it?"

"They always do it. All you have to do is mention New York."

"What happened to her?"

"She had a nervous breakdown and joined EST. Nine years later she came out again and apologized. But that's a long time to wait, nine formative years."

Yeah he'd make it a double session but only charge her for one. Or was that too Pavlovian and unprofessional?

You're not supposed to let your patients know that you like them, he remembered. It's that fucking blank slate.

"What can you do to feel better?" Doc asked.

"My last lover's boyfriend got to go to her mother's house whenever he wanted to. He got to go so much that he didn't want to anymore. He even got to go when they were breaking up so she could be with me. But I never got to go."

"Oh," Doc said. "That is not right."

"Soon it will be my birthday and I want to go."

"I think you should go," Doc said.

"Her mother has an apartment on the Upper West Side. I want to go there."

"Do you have the address?"

"Yes, I called information and got listings for everyone with that name on the Upper West Side, and I narrowed it down to her."

"How are you going to get there?"

By this time Anna's body language was entirely different. That's because she was scheming, strategizing for things to go her way.

"I'm going to wake up on the morning of my birthday. I'm going to put on my best clothes. I'm going to take the subway, and when I get out I'll go to the nearest Korean fruit stand and buy some flowers. Some special flowers. Some orange ones. Then I'll go to her door and ring the buzzer."

"What if there's a doorman?" Doc said. "They have those on the Upper West Side, you know."

"If there's a doorman, I'll announce myself. I'll say 'I've come to bring some flowers.' I'll get the best ones."

"Even if they're expensive?"

"It's my birthday," Anna said. "I don't care how much it costs."

There was a pause then, common among patients, and Doc took advantage of it to look out the window. He always noticed these shifts in conversation that seemed to be physical ones. They had to do with breathing.

"But Anna, what if she doesn't let me in, I mean, let *you* in?"

"I don't know," Anna said.

There was another one, a shift. When a person walks on a dark road at night and no light, there's a bouncing slide and dry smell. Then, let's say, the road becomes asphalt. It's obvious, the change.

"What do you think, Doc?"

"Well," he said. "Why do you need her mother to let you in the house?"

"I need it because I am not slime. I need it because I am good enough to invite for dinner."

"Well then," he said very upset, "well then, I think you're doing the right thing."

Chapter Eleven

Doc sat thoughtfully, looking out the window.

Five years ago this neighborhood was gentrified, he thought. *There were strangers everywhere buying art that no residents could afford or understand. There were no more pet shops or used refrigerator stores or TV repair.*

Now, thanks to thousands of drug addicts defecating in hallways and the stock market crash, rents had gone down. Thanks to drugs it was a slum again. Stores only opened if they sold something cheap like Pepsi or shampoo.

There were never pictures of the Depression paraded in the newspapers anymore. And they were probably no longer displayed casually on television specials as symbols of the past. Doc didn't have a television but he could predict that sort of thing. He just didn't need one. He could always tell what was on TV when he heard more than two people in a row say the same strange phrase in the same way. He knew that they had just seen it on television. A few weeks later everyone would have those words written on their chests. When he needed a program he just went for a walk.

The stairs. The door. The steps. The street. That's how it went. Then he'd be shocked at how sweet the cherry blossoms smelled, right in the middle of all that junk. Why were there blossoms of anything in February? A sound. A dog. A woman with a beard. Two running nuns. A secondhand shoe. The sadness of being alone in the house for a while. The way the rain smells any time of year.

"I want to get these images out of the freezer," Doc said later, safely back at home. "I mean, the ice."

He needed to sit around. Then he had to eat. He had to. He was embarrassed by eating. He knew he wasn't doing it right. It was the wrong thing or the wrong way. It was supposed to be a socializing habit. Doc made a whole salad and then was too tired to take even one bite. So he had a corn muffin-salad-mayonnaise sandwich instead. No toaster. No microwave. No toaster oven. No electricity, remember? His practice was going well enough for basic necessities but that did not include repairs. The fridge was plugged into the living room but without kitchen-based electricity, the appliance question was moot.

The minute the last piece of food was off the plate he started walking, chewing toward the sink to get it out of the way. He was angry because it wasn't right or enough. So, Doc took out his green box of recipes and started flipping through the index cards. He dropped it often, so they were not in very good order.

Sweet Potato Cheesecake, Baked Dip and Shake Chicken for Seven, Chicken-a-la-Mac, Chicken-a-la-Orange, Chicken Parisienne, Chicken and Rice Scrapple, Oven-Fried Chicken Drumsticks, Shrimp Bites for Six, Spaghetti with Pork sauce.

Some of the sections had headings like PIE.

> PIE:
>
> Chicken-Vegetable Pie, Chili-Hominy Pie, Deviled Ham and Cheese Pie, Double Corn and Meat Pie, Egg Custard Pie, Frozen Pumpkin Ice Cream Pie, Jell-O Pecan Pie, Peanutty Crunch Pie for Eight, Peppermint Pie, Potato-topped Hamburger Pie, Sausage-Beef Pie, Yam Pie.

Under VEGETABLES there were

VEGETABLES
French-Fried Rutabagas, Curried Succotash, Squash Bean Boats.

He decided to read some ingredients.

THOUSAND ISLAND DRESSING

1 cup mayonnaise
2 Tbl chili sauce
⅓ cup milk
2 Tbl sweet pickle relish
1 chopped hard-boiled egg

Combine ingredients and stir.

Doc noticed how white his legs were. Thanks to the ozone people couldn't sit in the sun anymore. Caucasians had always been the ugliest race and now there was really no way out.

FRENCH DRESSING

1 cup Hellman's mayonnaise
½ cup Mazola corn oil
¾ Tbl sugar
⅓ cup wine vinegar
1 Tbl dry mustard

Beat oil into mayonnaise. Add remaining ingredients. Combine and stir.

SPAM PATIO DIP

3 oz Spam
½ cup sour cream
1 ½ tsp horseradish

Stir.

Then he looked under DESSERTS.

DESSERTS:
Berry-Merry Sweets, Choco-Mocha Sponge and Snow.

This food meant so much. It came from the most dangerous magazine in the United States of America, *Family Circle*.

THREE MUSKETEERS TREASURE PUFFS

1 pkg quick crescent dinner rolls	*2 Three Musketeers bars*

Separate dough into triangles. Place a piece of bar on each triangle. Wrap around candy, completely covering it. Squeeze edges tightly to seal. Bake at 370 degrees until golden brown. Serve warm.

This was special food. Food intended for special family occasions. It came from the time when America had dreams. When Americans didn't mind being geeky and weird because soon the whole world would be that way too. It didn't mind eating slop because America would make slop important. Slop would have meaning. Slop would mean power.

Whatever happened to upward mobility? Doc suddenly remembered. It only seemed to apply to immigrants from very poor countries and even then they had to work twenty-four hours a day for one or two entire generations. It seemed virtually impossible for anyone else to become richer than their parents no matter how hard they tried. It didn't change if they were CEOs or on the welfare roles. All the children were worse off.

Then Doc remembered that he had been promised video telephones by 1980. He forgot why.

Doc put the slop out of his mind and cancer, its logical conclusion. Instead he went to buy a scoop of ice cream at the corner store.

God, their flavors were really complicated. They were all based on muddy combinations like Chocolate Super Fudge Crunch Raspberry Swirl. Or else it was allusions to popular culture, like Cherry Garcia. If you weren't a Grateful Dead fan, you wouldn't know what you were eating.

"Excuse me," Doc asked the clerk politely. "Don't you have any ice cream with only one word in the title? And one without any sexual innuendo please."

Later, at home between patients, the phone rang.

"Doctor's office."

"Anna O. here."

"Anna."

"Doc, will you come with me? We'll make it session number three."

He felt sore in various places.

"Anna, if you want me to come you'll have to pay my full rate."

"Ten bucks an hour!"

"That's right. You know I'm going to be spending the whole time listening to you talk."

"Thank you, Doctor. This is going to be my greatest birthday, ever. Thank you, Doctor. Thank you."

Chapter Twelve

Anna was flipping through the newspaper, bored at a receptionist job. Being a true New Yorker she had always turned first to the obituaries. It was a well-worn habit left over from when that was the only way to get an apartment. But now it helped her keep up with her friends.

Oh shit, she said. *Jack died.*

Jack died and Anna missed it.

She'd last seen him walking down the block the spring before. No, it was warm but it wasn't spring. The cherry blossoms bloom too early now. It must have been February.

"Anna!"

"Jack, how are you doing?"

"Well, Tim is dying."

"Yes."

Jack was really short. He had fiery red hair and dirt on his shirt.

"Yeah, Anna. He was just on *Good Morning America* two weeks ago and seemed so immortal. Now he's got lesions on his lungs. I want to see him every day but you know how Tim is. He has to entertain. I've never officially said good-bye to anyone before.

Jack was smiling through all of this. His manner was conversational.

"The thing is, Anna, it's all getting so normal. I mean, the first group that died – well, they didn't even know what was happening to them. Then the second group was all waiting for the miracle cure around the corner – Q, Ampligen, egg whites, bloodfreezing, aspirin. Running around from doctor to doctor trying anything. But this group – we all know it's probable death. There's no mystery anymore, no romance. There's no way out. I mean, ten years ago if some thirty-three-year-old fellow died, his whole friendship circle would be devastated for years. They'd never get over it. Now it's so normal to die at thirty-two. We abandon them when they're halfway into that purgatory between home and hospital. We don't even wait around for them to die anymore – too many others standing in line. Last night I walked into a room where a quarter of the men had lesions on their faces. Some had small lesions, peeking through thinning hairlines like a little kiss from God. Others had those big porous oozing ones. My black friends' lesions are black. They were walking around with lesions holding little cocktail glasses and flirting. Oh men, they can't admit to being frail, even when running back and forth between the flirt and their diarrhea. Now Tim's dying. And his dying is so different from Phil's dying. Vito left instructions for his memorial service – he picked out which Judy Garland clips should be shown. John Bernd went so long ago now."

"You've been to a lot of funerals, haven't you?" Anna asked.

"Oh, Anna, you don't know the half of it. I've been to so many AIDS funerals I haven't been doing much of anything else. I've been to funerals of mediocre people who were eulogized as geniuses, funerals of geniuses where there was no one adequate to eulogize them. I've been to open and closed caskets, funerals where you have to get there an hour early to grab a seat, and funerals that no one else cared to see. I've been there when there's so much Jesus Christ you can't even find the corpse. I've been to funerals where anyone could speak and funerals where only famous people could speak. Funerals where the speaker blamed the death on the mourners, funerals where the speakers praised the mourners for fighting death. The way you reacted when I told you Tim is dying, will you be that casual when it is my turn?"

"No," she said. "I will cry and cry."

And she did.

These are the simple facts of death, Anna thought later when the immediate sadness had faded. She was shocked at how easily it could be accepted. She was shocked to have so many dead friends at the age of thirty-one. When she was a girl, many people thought that Americans would live forever. They ate breakfast squares and freeze-dried orange juice just like those fucking astronauts. They reserved places on the first civilian shuttle to the moon. Earth didn't matter then. We could always go somewhere else. Nowadays, most people wonder if they'll ever get old. Living becomes an obsession. A dream.

Chapter Thirteen

Doc was sitting up one morning eating his cold Pop-Tarts. Here it was, April and already summer. It was summer again while people could still remember the last one. They started killing each other immediately and getting very irritated. Something about the wanton brutality made Doc associate freely to that damn woman in the white leather.

Embraces remembered or still vaguely hoped for.

"Oh no," Doc said. "This is a memory that is too much to take. It is the illusion of something that no longer exists but still should exist."

Trying to escape this melancholy manifestation, Doc went back further in his mind, flipping through images until he could relax with a benign one and watch between commercials. Nostalgia is so much more palatable than real feeling.

Okay, there were certain truths he couldn't face. But there was still some comfort for Doc when he remembered, from time to time, that he was basically a nice person. It was all because he listened. He listened when people spoke so he knew what they cared about and what they needed. Without listening there is no love. There is nothing. Doc knew this. He hated interrupters. He despised them. They don't let other people say their words. They lock them up. They stop them every time. Just like that woman in the white leather.

What did she have that made me feel so much?

(There are so many inadequate responses to a question of this nature. It is hard to see the precise shapes of things. The precisely stacked boxes of air and boxy trucks that bring *The New York Times*. It's hard to sum up those people who pass you on escalators. Some people have sex by putting fishhooks in each other. Couple this act with a simple understanding of the basic function of all living creatures to expand and contract. Now, try that with fishhooks.)

But there was still more to listening. It can't simply be waiting until the other person is finished before *you* talk. Listening means not having something to say back until after they've told you everything. Even if the other spoke in code, all Doc had to do was take it slow. For example, if someone said,

"I just shot up heroin,"

Doc knew that they had just shot up heroin.

Doc looked out the window. Sometimes in his imagination a bad person did good things and was redeemed. But was the bad person actually Doc himself, awaiting another's benevolence? Or was the bad person someone else, and so he'd have to forgive her? It was so hard to know/decide. If only they could talk things over for a minute so he could remember how awful she really was.

Doc had a dream. Three white people were standing on a street corner. All were junkies. One, a man, had shot up so many times that there were bleeding track marks and needle pricks in his arm. There was an inadequate bandage soaked in blood. He was standing in casual conversation with another drug addict who held a bloody syringe. A third was staggering toward them, on the nod, finally impacting his arm on the other's needle.

At first Doc thought it had something to do with penetration. That was how he had been trained to think about things. But after some time it became clear to him that using drug addicts as metaphors was perfectly natural since they were a normal part of his environment. It would be like someone in Nebraska dreaming about the plains. Then he realized that this was a dream about three different states. About having too much. About having something to give.

About being in need. When it came to listening, of course, Doc was all three of these people.

He recalled an instance of failed listening.

DOC

I'm leaving you because you don't listen.

THE WOMAN IN WHITE LEATHER

You left me because you think my artwork stinks. You left me because of your mother. You left me because you won't stay in the relationship for the good and the bad.

To Doc, this was a litany of diversions. Why would this lady in leather project all of her imagined deficiencies onto a situation where all she really needed to do was be quiet? Apparently she preferred to be completely despised over simply paying attention. What was she afraid to hear? What was it?

Doc proposed another alternative for this scenario.

DOC

I'm leaving you because you don't listen.

THE WOMAN IN WHITE LEATHER

(Silence.)

Silence is the constructive response when being told you don't listen.

(*Silence*.)

Then Doc would propose.

WOMAN IN WHITE LEATHER

I'm sorry I didn't listen.

Then she would simply do it. She would let Doc say every word without being rushed. She would let him have a long time to say it. She would not be planning her rebuttal all along. She would ask clarifying questions, not trick ones. But she would only be able to do that if she really wanted to know. If she didn't really want to know it wasn't love. If it was, she would have listened and then she and Doc could stay together.

Chapter Fourteen

"Happy Birthday," he said to Anna O., but she didn't look very happy.

"I just came from my friend Jack's memorial service," she said.

"How was it?"

"It was okay. Actually, I really had to smile because Jack was such a control queen that he planned how *we* would memorialize *him*. In fact there was even a moment when we had to sit and listen to Jack's favorite songs. He made us listen to Steely Dan."

"What food did he pick?"

"Coffee and danish. When his mother stood up to speak I was really worried because that is everybody's nightmare – to die and your mother has the last word. But actually, it turned out that she really knew him. Mostly at these services the parent never knew their child."

"What are you remembering about him right now?"

"You know, Jack really did not want to give up fucking. And when he decided to give it up he was very, very sad. He had let someone fuck him without a condom and they had talked about it later for an hour and a half. Each one saying that it was the other one's responsibility. Jack said that because he was being fucked, he wanted to give over completely and leave the other guy in charge. The other guy said that because Jack was the one taking it, it was Jack's responsibility to protect himself. After that Jack gave up fucking. I think the hardest sex act in the world to live without would be oral sex. Doing it, I mean. What about for you, Doc?"

"Kissing."

"Well, if kissing spread AIDS we would all jump off the cliff. What's that, a bomb?"

"No, Anna, it's your birthday present. Happy birthday."

It was wrapped and thoughtful. It made her happy. Doc could tell. Presents make people happy if they are given with caring. They require some forethought.

"Oh, Torah Personality Cards, my favorite."

"They're pictures of famous Torah scholars," he explained. "Hasidic boys trade them like baseball cards ... probably."

Then they headed down into the subway and had a seat. Well, it wasn't quite as easy as all that. By the street entrance to the train there were seven people asking for money. There were people standing by the token line asking for money. There were people by turnstiles asking for money. Once through the turnstiles, there were people on the platform asleep or staring, urinating and stinking of rotting flesh. When the train came and Doc and Anna took their seats, it was the Motel A Train. The A had the longest route in the system and so the guests can take the longest naps.

While they were sitting, a number of people came by selling *Street News*, but none of the passengers wanted to buy it because savvy New Yorkers knew that it was a scam. It had no articles about the street. It was just a way for a publisher to sell his paper without having to pay minimum wage. Then another bunch of homeless came through selling copies of the *Daily News*, which had been on strike for months and months. The bosses, not being dumb, distributed the strike-breaking copies free to homeless people, who immediately tried to resell them, making themselves de facto scabs. Now, this situation really tested Doc's sensibility. He had to decide which was more moral – buying a paper from a homeless person or not buying it.

"Ladies and gentlemen," the man said, pointing to a knife scar on his chest. "I got this wound from a mortar shrapnel in a battle on

Christmas night, right outside of Kim Lee."

"What kind of Vietnamese name is Kim Lee?" Anna asked.

"I think it's a Chinese restaurant on Fourteenth Street," Doc said.

"At Jack's service this morning," Anna continued, as though all of this was normal, "I realized that when I first comprehended the enormity of what was happening to my community, I only anticipated that I would lose many people. But, I did not understand that those of us who remain, that is to say, those of us who will continue to lose and lose, would also lose our ability to fully mourn. I feel that I have been dehumanized by the quantity of death, and that now I can no longer fully grieve each person. How much I loved them and how much I miss them. Doc, you know that expression Silence=Death?"

"Yeah," Doc said.

"I'm beginning to realize that at the same time that that is true, Voice does not necessarily equal Life."

By this time the beggar had finished up with their car, having collected about a dollar. He put his shirt back on, like he was backstage and preparing for his next entrance.

"Do you ever think about leaving New York?" Anna asked.

"What does that mean?" Doc said.

"Oh," Anna sighed. "You're one of those."

Doc cleared his throat, trying not to pry.

"Do *you* ever think about leaving New York, Anna?"

"Well, there is always San Francisco. There are a lot of women there and my parents are here. I was visiting once and I went swimming in one of those great public pools they have there."

"Public pools?" Doc asked, amazed. "That actually work?"

"Yeah, and locker rooms full of dykes. They are all there undressing and redressing very slowly in front of each other. I just sat down on a bench and watched this one. When she left she threw me a great smile. Gay people are normal there. There's no shame."

"Why don't you move?" Doc asked.

"What? And give up my shame? Don't you think it would get boring?"

"Look at that," Doc said, pointing to a public service announcement hanging in the ad strip over the windows. "When I was a kid they told us not to cross in the middle of the block. Now it says DON'T SHARE NEEDLES."

But Anna sighed again.

"Let's chat," he said, getting back to work. "Let's chat before we reach our destination."

"About what?"

"Tell me about ... a different relationship. The one before this one. Tell me about someone before Miss Bitch. How about the one from the small town in Pennsylvania?"

"Not that one, Doc, I wouldn't know what to say."

"Well, how about the opera singer?"

"Too painful."

"The one from the Bronx?"

"God, you're a great listener, Doc, to remember all those details."

"Thanks. Let's look at an old relationship so we can see if there are any patterns that you may want to look into on your own at some future time."

"It's a long story."

"Well, the train seems to be stopped between stations, so I guess I have the time."

"Thank you," she said. "Being uncomfortable is being away but I feel okay because I know you're listening. And no matter what goes on when I think alone, Doc, it is always different to announce it."

"I'm listening," he said.

Chapter Fifteen

"I used to waitress at this place called Captain Mike's Seafood Restaurant right near City Hall. I made between two-fifty and three hundred a week, so it was a good job. My girlfriend's name was Lucy and she used to live in Indonesia. Ever since I met her she wanted to go back and visit. So, every week I put fifty dollars into the Dry Dock Savings Bank, scrimped on everything, and when I had enough saved up to make the trip, I quit.

The flight time was too long. First it took eight hours to get to Amsterdam and then twenty-four more to get to Djakarta, with stopovers in Frankfurt, Rome, Abu Dhabi, and Bangkok. The major event of every international airport is that they're all the same. There are duty-free shops in all of them and they all have the same stuff. There are former colonials in all the duty-free shops and they all like to smoke in the no-smoking section. Lucy and I survived the trip and were still friends. At two-thirty a.m. Abu Dhabi time I asked her what Indonesia was like.

'It's hot and very beautiful,' she said.

'But, I mean, what's happening there?' I said. 'What are the current questions?'

'I don't know how to describe it,' Lucy said.

We got off in Djakarta and stepped into this incredible heat. We were in it. There were loud motorbikes and clove cigarettes. The city had these massive dull white buildings, half postmodern Moslem, half Hyatt hotel. They stick up here and there. People jump onto overflowing double-decker buses. Entire families get on one zooming

Honda bike. There are people in sarongs, in blue jeans, selling fried bananas and TDK receivers. One thousand rupiah equals one dollar. The hotel room cost five thousand including fan, mosquito net, and papaya. Our first meal of Nasi Goreng with hot sauce and shrimp cracker was sixty cents. I took out my Indonesian phrase book.

'The people here are so beautiful,' Lucy said.

'Yeah,' I said. 'Some of them are very beautiful. How do you pronounce this, Apu *Ka*bar or Apu Ka*bar*?'

'I don't know,' she said. 'What does it mean?'

'*How are you*. Didn't you learn any Indonesian during the year that you stayed here?'

'Not really,' she said. 'The family I lived with spoke English.'

'Oh.'

It started getting dark and we were walking along the railroad tracks. We were in a slum, I guess. There were lots of small shacks crowded together, garbage everywhere, naked children, and howling, mangy, mongrel dogs. Every other shack had a TV set. It was like Avenue C with no winter and not being afraid of your neighbor.

We walked along until a kid came up and said, 'Hello, mister.'

'Hello, mister,' said another kid.

'Hello, mister.'

'They think we're men,' I said.

'No,' Lucy answered. 'They think that means *hello*.'

'I guess there have been too many misters here,' I said.

The next day we took a thirteen-hour train trip across Java to Surabaja – eighteen thousand rupiah for second-class with air-conditioning. Third-class sat on bamboo benches sweating, and the last car carried refrigerators and color TVs. In Surabaja there was a stifling two-hour wait for the bus so we ate some more Nasi Goreng and smoked clove cigarettes.

'That man looks so much like Mansur,' Lucy said. 'So many men here remind me of him. I have to be firm with his family and tell them as honestly as possible that I am not going to marry him and I'm not going to Australia to visit him. I wonder if we can extend our return tickets. I love it here so much I want to stay forever.'

The bus ride was nine hours to Denpasar including a lunch stop for Nasi Goreng and a Kung Fu movie shown on the bus's TV. It was a reject film called *Gambling for Head* from Hong Kong in English with Indonesian subtitles. The bus stopped when the film was playing so the driver could watch it too. The whole time I was thinking about Vietnam and how hot it must have been, how totally hot for those guys in uniforms with pounds of equipment. How hot with no relief.

After the bus we rode the ferry, standing on the front deck staring down the mountains of Bali, and suddenly we were there. We were in Bali where people put dried flowers on the street and the shrines were wrapped in cloth and jasmine burned. We drove from the dock in a bus to the terminal which was chaotic. Even before stepping out into the crowd we were surrounded by van drivers.

'Bimo.'

'Taxi.'

'Charter.'

'Minibus.'

'Kuta.'

'Kuta, five thousand.'

Lucy bartered to three thousand and rode along relaxed but I couldn't help noticing that all the Indonesian riders paid two hundred.

The bimo drivers posed with their cigarettes like American movie stars. They leaned back into their tight, tight jeans and flashed practiced *I know you want to fuck me* smiles. I understood it all better later, walking down main street on Kuta Beach surrounded by white girls clinging to Indonesian men, zipping by on their motor bikes.

There was something grotesque about Kuta. There were shops with Italian fashions. There were beer gardens advertising drinking competitions. There were swarms of sunburnt Australians wearing I HAD A BALL IN BALI T-shirts.

'Isn't it fun?' Lucy said.

We found a hotel for three thousand and went back out on the street. Someone handed us a flyer.

CELEBRATE NEW YEAR'S EVE AT CASABLANCA

A REAL AUSSIE BAR

BEST LEGS IN KUTA COMPETITION AT MIDNIGHT

Eventually we figured out that that very night was the Hindu New Year, as crowds started to gather along the streets waiting and talking until drums started banging, gunpowder exploding, and a parade of giant paper monsters came marching down the street.

'Come on,' Lucy said, pulling me off in the opposite direction toward a field behind the beach. 'Mansur showed me a guy who hung out here with a cow. He had great Buddha sticks for five thousand. I know it's been years but maybe he's still there.'

We walked through an empty field looking for drugs and found nothing. Then Lucy took me back to the street, down an alley, and into a tiny bamboo restaurant, empty except for a parrot. Everyone else could be heard in the background cheering the puppets, clanging and stamping, chasing away evil spirits.

'Mansur took me here. They sell psychedelic mushroom soup.'

But the woman sweating out the New Year shift said the police had cracked down long ago on the magic side of Bali and there was no more blue mushroom soup in Kuta. As a last resort Lucy went to the Casablanca to look for likely dopers, preferably twenty-year-old Australian boys who seemed manageable.

'Do you know where we can get some smoke?'

'I can get you cocaine,' two different bearded dudes said. 'But no smoke. There isn't any more. Besides you're better off not asking because they'll sell it to you and then turn you in.'

One New Zealander with a STONED AGAIN T-shirt warned her to give up the idea completely.

'My friend just got eleven months for buying three thousand worth. Just have a beer. It's cheap.'

The next morning the sun was full by five-thirty. There were roosters, dogs, and, naturally, backlit green palm leaves. There were enormous red and yellow flowers. Lucy and I sat underneath them to drink the tea and bananas left out by the manager. Then we prepared to walk down to the beach. The cabin's steps were covered with dried flowers and burning jasmine.

'Where are you going?' asked the manager.

'To the beach.'

'No good,' he said. 'No good to go outside today. Today is silent day in Bali. No go out. No electricity.'

So we sat peacefully and dutifully in our room, sweating, watching through the window as the sun got hotter and hotter. We sang songs and made love and took endless showers in the *mandi* and finally, after eight hours of blistering heat and carefully rationing out a can of mackerel and some leftover stroop waffles from the Amsterdam airport, the sky began to cool and get darker through those same huge palm leaves and the same red and yellow flowers.

The next morning we decided to go to the beach again before setting out to find Lucy's Indonesian friend Dorothy. Ten minutes into our walk to the water, my shoulders started sizzling. I could hear them. Then I had this small realization. I realized that this trip was an exercise in which I would take Lucy's description of people and things and match them with the reality, thereby learning more about her than I ever could at home.

This guy came up to me and said, 'Hello, I love you. You want a bikini, cheap?'

'Hello,' I said. 'No thank you.'

Then another guy. 'Hello, where do you come from?'

'New York.'

'Then another guy. 'Silver, silver.'

'No thank you.'

'Very cheap.'

'No thank you.'

Then another guy. 'Hello.'

'No, nothing. No thank you.'

'Hello, where do you come from?'

'Look,' Lucy said, turning toward the water. 'How beautiful.'

The beach was wide and hot and bordered that blue Pacific. Australians surfed. Germans tanned in their string bikinis and Japanese swam in their fluorescent trunks. It was so hot that the sand stung through my sneakers. Neither of us had bathing suits so we each took turns going in in our underwear while the other guarded the stuff. I dove in.

Then it was Lucy's turn.

As I sat watching her wade out, a skinny dark woman came over in a sarong and T-shirt that said KUTA MASSAGE TEAM.

'Massage?'

'No thank you.'

'Good massage, cheap.'

'No thank you.'

'Bikinis?'

'No thank you. Nothing. I don't want anything.'

'Listen, I'll give you a cheap price.' The woman sat down on the sand and started unloading a pile of polyester T-shirts that read I'VE BEEN IN BALI TOO.

'No, nothing. I don't want anything.'

'Look,' she said, holding up a hot-pink crocheted bikini. 'Only ten thousand. I'll give you a good price.'

'I don't want anything. I don't want anything. I don't want anything. No thank you.'

'Okay, what you pay? What's your last offer? Nine thousand?'

'No, I didn't even make a first offer. I don't want anything.'

'American very rich, much money. Seven thousand.'

But I didn't want a pink bikini and I'm not rich and I would never buy anything for more than five dollars anyway. I buy all my clothes at the Salvation Army. But I ended up with a hideous blue and gray belt worth twenty-five cents at Lamston's. I paid one thousand.

'Lucy, thank God you're back.'

Just as she sat down to dry in the sun, I heard another voice behind me.

'Silver?'

'No, I don't want anything. Please go away. I don't want anything. No.'

'Why you no buy?' he said, squatting down so close I could feel his breath.

'Because I don't want anything.'

'You must buy. You have money. We need blue jeans, forty thousand. Just one ring.'

'No, really. I don't want a ring.'

'I love you,' he said. 'I love you.'

All this time Lucy was sitting about one yard away, staring at the sea in her baggy sandy underpants. I ran into the water and he didn't talk to her at all, just moved on to a Swiss couple farther down the beach. I knew they weren't German. It didn't take long in Kuta to learn to tell a German by his string bikini.

That night I sat waiting in a restaurant while Lucy finished putting on her makeup. At the next table was a fashionable, clean-cut Japanese man dressed exactly like a fashionable clean-cut American man circa 1962. Only now that look has come back. You know, the nerd look. Tortoiseshell eyeglasses, khaki Bermuda shorts, and white sneakers.

'You like Bali?'

'Some things are beautiful. Some things are not so beautiful.'

'Oooh,' he said, nodding his head. 'Bali is *baguse*.' And he held up his thumb.

Then I understood why there was Hotel Baguse and Café Baguse and thousands of T-shirts worn by tourists and Indonesians alike all saying "BAGUSE." It means *cool.* And the main message of Bali's public relations is that Bali is cool.

'You could say that,' I answered, and then turned to my copy of *The Djakarta Post.*

According to the front page, two ganja dealers had been sentenced to ten years each. The government was cracking down on factories that hired women for night work without their husband's permission. A court sentenced two Indonesians to four years in prison for instigating anti-Chinese riots resulting in the deaths of nine Chinese. The paper expressed outrage at these 'extreme' sentences.

Lucy came to the table then and we looked at the menu. The only Indonesian dish was Nasi Goreng. The other options were submarine sandwich, T-bone steak, and pizza. The waiter sat down at our table to take the order because it was too hot to stand.

'Where do you come from?'

'America,' I said. 'Where do you come from?'

'Java. Jojokarta. I'm a painter. See my paintings on the wall? I teach batik class. You like Bali?'

'It's complicated,' I said. 'Everywhere they advertise that Bali is *baguse*, but I think Bali is ...'

'Bullshit,' he said and leaned back in the bamboo chair.

The next morning at six a.m. we started looking for Dorothy. After endless haggling with bimos and endless consultations with people about the return address on Lucy's crumpled envelope, we ended up walking a bunch of unshaded kilos along a country road.

'I met her on the ferry from Java, the first time,' Lucy said. 'She invited me to her house and I stayed there for a year. Mansur was a friend of the family.'

'What's she like?'

The sun was stomping down on our heads. I could barely breathe, like I was trapped in a vacuum-sealed jar.

'Hello, mister.'

'Hello, mister. Give me money.'

'I don't know her that well,' Lucy said.

'Lucy, you've lived with her for a long time. You must know something.'

The rice fields rang with a cacophony of 'Hello, mister's.

'She's a very generous woman,' Lucy said. 'Her husband works in a big hotel in Sanur. She is very kind and very religious. I think of her as one of my closest friends. She had three daughters. I love those kids so much. She used to live in the city. Now she has moved to the country.'

The road was all dirt by this time. Almost a footpath.

'She sure has,' I said. 'This is pretty rural.'

I looked out over the rice fields at the farmers in thatched huts and sarongs and all those palm trees. It reminded me of every movie I'd ever seen about Vietnam.

'The only time I've ever seen scenery like this is right before it gets firebombed.'

'What?'

'Nothing.'

'Hello, mister. Give me money.'

Everyone standing by the side of the road noticed us and most of the children said 'Hello, mister.' The only ones who paid no attention at all were the shirtless old women carrying bowls of grain on their heads. They didn't scowl or show scorn. They were simply disinterested. Maybe they were the independence generation. People who know what's wrong with the West.

Kids were following us the whole time and I could smell my own flesh broiling. After another hour of fields, sheds, and old houses, we turned a bend and came upon a project of brand-new homes, all white and alike with identical garden plots and red-tiled roofs.

'There she is, the oldest girl. There's Nofri,' Lucy said. The kids called out her name and ran toward us. Soon we were led into the house by clinging children to meet Dorothy in her Peggy Fleming haircut, Australian makeup, and pedal pushers. She showed us the house.

'We bought it this year,' she said, showing off the three bedrooms, two living rooms, sit-down kitchen, and tiled *mandi*. 'It's a new settlement here.'

Each room was furnished with sturdy new wardrobes, couches, and armchairs. The lush garden was being cared for by a young boy, while another servant, a young woman, washed dishes in the back. The children wore starched, sparkling Western clothing, and there were two new motorbikes parked outside.

'Presents,' Nofri said, patting Lucy's bag.

'Tomorrow,' Lucy said.

'*Besok*,' I said, remembering it from my Indonesian phrase book. Something felt very wrong in the way we were interacting with everyone.

Dorothy and her husband, Cholid, rode Lucy and I back to the hotel on their motorbikes, insisting that we come the next day to stay with them. But when we got to the hotel's courtyard, Dorothy wrinkled up her nose.

'I no like,' she said. 'Cheap. Dirty.'

'Oh no,' Lucy said. 'It's fine for us.'

Dorothy spoke to her husband in Indonesian.

'I know,' she said. 'Mansur brought you to this place.'

'No,' Lucy said.

'Mansur tell me he stay with you at the Bali Hyatt and you pay for it.'

'Hyatt? No, never. I can't afford that.'

But Dorothy wasn't listening.

Later I told Lucy, 'Dorothy thinks you're rich.'

'I could never make her understand that,' she said. 'Or Mansur. Whenever we spent the night together he expected me to pay for everything.'

The next day we followed Dorothy's directions for an easier way to her house and went through Denpasar, passing lots of teenage boys selling cassettes of American rock bands. There was also a cinema showing four Clint Eastwood movies.

'Presents,' screamed Nofri when we arrived. Three-dollar watches from Canal Street for the girls and Western dresses for Dorothy.

'These are from the shop where I work,' said Lucy. 'I got them on discount. *Discount*.'

'In America, much money,' Dorothy said, stepping out of one dress and trying on another. 'But then my friends from America or Holland or Germany send me money and I can buy rice. If my friend have nothing and I have only one thousand, I give him five hundred.'

The maid brought in the washing.

'In America you have much money. You eat in restaurant.'

I came to an ad in the Australian magazine. It was for Courvoisier. A man in a tux and woman in a gown drank cognac under the smile of a white-jacketed waiter.

'Lucy, how much rent you pay, one month?'

'Three hundred dollars.'

'I pay five hundred for a whole year. America – much money. Maybe you send me a plastic raincoat.'

'What color?' Lucy sighed.

'You choose,' Dorothy said, sitting back with a smile.

Sleeping in Dorothy's house we couldn't touch or kiss because it was too hot to close the door.

'You know, Lucy,' I said. 'Dorothy could be a nouveau riche housewife in any suburb in the world.'

'Tomorrow I must see Mansur's brother,' she said, 'and tell him I'm not going to marry Mansur. First thing tomorrow.'

Mansur's brother, Ansar, lived in an older part of Denpasar, behind the bimo terminal. He owned his own home too and lived there with his wife, mother, and three children. Lucy said he used to be a playboy until he got a woman pregnant and had to marry her. Now he's a salesman for Hobart restaurant equipment.

We ate dinner there in front of the TV and then retired to the living room to listen to Julio Iglesias sing "Begin the Beguine" in Spanish on Ansar's Pioneer tape deck. Palm trees grew outside but the living room was decorated with plastic ones and a bowl of plastic papayas.

'Here in Indonesia, I work and work and never get anything,' he said. 'In Melbourne, my brother makes money.'

His wife brought in sirop and cakes. A servant washed dishes in the background.

'I have not heard from Mansur in about one year. He sent a picture of himself working in a fruit market.'

There was the picture. Mansur smiled in his Aussie clothing, leaning on a crate of lemons.

'He changed his name now, to Mark Starr. Better for Australia. Whenever he talk, Lucy, he talk about you. I know everything. Everything. I had an American girlfriend too. A long time ago. Now she works for Federico Fellini. I want everything for my brother that I never had.'

We drank some more sirop until another man came into the house. He had darker skin and whiter clothes, a Muslim cap and a brighter face. Abdul was cool. He wasn't depressed. He didn't want blue jeans.

'You see,' he said, 'I've been in the West, man. I've been in Thailand and Germany. I've played in the snow, man. I know the West. I understand. It's great to travel but Bali is my home. It's quiet here. I can stay in my house, I can look at the stars, I can eat cakes. Everyone knows me. You can go down to Kuta and say "Hello from Abdul" and everyone will smile. I know there's nothing better over there than everyone has here. I've seen it so now I can relax.'

And I was really glad to hear that, someone who knew the truth. Someone with perspective. Someone smart enough to sit back and sip sirop and listen to music and know that that's something. But Ansar kind of laughed at him, like one of those former rockers in the suburbs who keeps an old hippie friend around just for old time's sake. Then Ansar got up to turn over the Julio Iglesias record and Abdul leaned over.

'You want junk?'

Finally it was time to go back to New York, and Lucy and I trudged silently to the airport. We were angry, not only because it was hot, but because they sent us to Building B where we were sent back to Building A where we were sent back to Building B, all the time carrying everything. Finally we went back to Building A and sat at the bar. I didn't even answer when the bartender asked, 'Where do you come from?'

I was sitting there thinking about the mountains that wind around the blue ocean and the monkeys just hanging out by the side of the road and the jackfruit and bananas everywhere. I thought about the children with painted lips and the sound of gamelan music all day long. And Lucy turned to me and said nothing. At that moment I saw her turn to me and I wanted her to say something that showed that she knew me. That she watched me. That she knew what kind of person I was. Not agree. I didn't need her to agree. Just notice. But I didn't get anything. Just a blank stare."

Chapter Sixteen

"We're there," she said. "This is the right stop." They got out together and walked down the platform.

"Wow," Doc said. "You were looking for morality and personal recognition in the middle of serious tourism. That's very *Heart of Darkness* of you. I mean, there's no way to be there and be polite because your presence itself is rude. But geographically, we're in the sphere of your humanity now. That's what is up for consideration. If this was the World Court, probably no one would care. But that's one of the strangest aspects of analysis, Anna. No one is looking at you but you. That, of course, has its ups and downs."

"I know, Doc, it's really confusing. I mean something different in the World than I mean in my world."

"You watch," he said meekly. "You listen when people talk. You listen too closely. You listen so closely to find the meaning that you never find the meaning."

"Not *the* meaning," she said. "But *a* meaning. If I look too closely I get these strange results that make it worth it. The same thing is true in love, Doc."

"How?"

"When a woman is really happy. When our faces are close and there is only streetlight, she looks slightly Mongoloid, her most beautiful. There's that way that she kisses when she really likes me. Too lightly on the forehead."

"Then you have to choose," Doc said, feeling slightly hurt, like there was some distasteful counter-transference going on. "You have to choose between your own vision and reciprocity. And remember, reciprocity is not on the general agenda for the nineties."

"Why not, Doc?"

"Because, Anna." *Thank God I got my authority back*, Doc thought. *Why do I want her to like me? That's supposed to be one of the advantages of being a man. I'm supposed to be able to have control and still slide around at the same time.*

"Because, Anna, most people don't listen to each other. They don't listen to themselves. They don't think about what other people mean and are feeling and the impact of their own words on others. They don't remember later what they said in the first place. They don't think about it when they're saying it. You listen too closely. You are overinformed. Do you want to have lunch first? What are you staring at?"

"Wow, Doc. This is very important to you, isn't it? Someone must have interrupted you big-time. You keep coming back to this listening thing over and over again."

Then she said, "Let's have lunch, buy the flowers, and get this over with."

Confidentially, it was Doc's birthday too, his thirty-first. He wished she would give him the flowers. Flowers. When they got out of the subway he made a phone call to an old number that he still remembered. He left a message on the tape asking something of this woman, asking this person who did not know how, to remember his birthday with kindness. It was a sneaky thing to do since Doc already knew what would happen. But he did it for reassurance of the status quo. However, once that tape actually beeped, he stammered, leaving uncertainty and weakness unretrievably on the answering machine. He had wanted to be careful, to not say one wrong word. Sometimes people jump on you for saying the wrong word. This woman in white was one of those people. If Doc said, "You know, I was thinking about going to San Francisco ..." then she would say, "What do you mean, *you know*? How am I supposed to know?"

She was always right down the other person's throat. She didn't listen to the intention behind the vocabulary. And whose fault was that?

They looked for a restaurant. The Upper West Side had a mystique about it that had not been deserved for some time. True, it had once been majestic, faded, with high ceilings, cheap apartments, huge rooms, Haitians, Dominicans, Holocaust survivors, student radicals, John Lennon, Leonard Bernstein, old women eating lunch. But it had lost its soul and become schlocky the way that rich people can. It had gotten greasy.

"What about this place?" Anna asked, pointing to a very normal, dirty leftover.

"No, not here," Doc said. "This is the kind of restaurant that is so disgusting the waitresses bring lunch from home and go to the coffee shop next door to use the bathroom."

"What about the coffee shop next door?"

"Okay."

"Forget it, Doc. I'm already nauseous. Let's go for a walk."

They walked around slowly.

"Now, Doc, family is a delicate thing. Families of lesbians are particularly hard."

They walked even slower.

"What is the most important thing to remember about families of lesbians?" Doc asked.

"That you just can't outwit them," Anna answered. "There's always some weird little twist. No matter how normal you try to be, you'll never be normal. Like last year my friend Nancy's mother died. It had been a long, horrible thing and we were all involved. On the morning of the funeral I started getting dressed. Suddenly I realized that all of these lesbians, Nancy's friends, were about to walk into a synagogue in South Brooklyn and Nancy wasn't even out to her relatives. It would be terrible for her."

"What would be terrible?"

"For them to see us as we truly are. And for them to see her for her."

"Why would that be terrible?"

"Because in their minds we are inherently terrible and she would, therefore, be punished emotionally. Better to pretend you're not what they think is terrible even though that's what you really are and even though you know it's not terrible – although somewhere else you do believe it's terrible – to avoid the emotional punishment."

"Got it."

"So, I decided to look as straight as I possibly can. I put on a beautiful black dress, designer stockings, shined my heels, makeup, two earrings from the same set. Then I got on the subway. An hour later, I climb out in the middle of nowhere and up ahead I see three of my friends. You know what? They all made the same decision. They all put on their best, most feminine clothing and they looked so beautiful. I loved them. We were walking together, our high heels clicking on the streets, our waists shapely, necks exposed and decorated. Then we stepped into the chapel and all Nancy's relatives were wearing polyester double knits. They couldn't stop staring. Later, at the shiva, her Uncle Heshy asked me if we were a rock and roll band. It's really hard to get away with being the wrong thing."

Then they bought the flowers. Seventeen dollars' worth.

"How do I look?"

"You look good, Anna. You look all dolled up."

"I've been in training for this for weeks. I've been swimming every day and doing yoga and running before work and only eating macrobiotic food and taking vitamins and not smoking. I went out shopping three times for the right dress and finally got this one for sixty-five dollars. That's a lot of word processing, let me tell you."

It was a serious dress.

"Maybe you're reliving something here," Doc said.

"Then I went and got a haircut and I tried on different lipsticks. I bought new heels. The prettier I look, the more she'll like me."

"Sounds like you're going to a funeral."

"You know, Doc, I did do this recently for another funeral. All my mother could say was 'Thank God you wore a dress. But your hair is too short.'"

"Yeah, I've got a mother like that too," he said.

"Look, Doc," Anna stopped short. "I just don't want her to take one look at me and say '*That dyke.*'"

"Who, your mother?"

"And my old lover's mother. None of them."

Crossing the streets took longer than either of them were used to because the avenues were so wide, but the lights changed more slowly so everything compensated.

"Doc, I promised myself this. I'm ready to do whatever it takes to get inside. If they have to call the police to stop me, let them call the police. Okay, Doc, wish me luck."

"Good luck," he said. Then he followed her into the building.

There was a doorman, just as Doc had predicted, and Doc watched him with suspicious anticipation. Would her disguise actually work? Anna announced herself with great dignity and grace and then the doorman phoned upstairs.

"Anna O. to see you," he said.

There was a sense of excitement as the doorman listened for a while.

"Thank you," he said into the phone.

"Sorry," he said to Anna, casually. Then he glanced suddenly to the left.

"What do you mean?"

He looked to the right, the way that all human beings do when they're uncomfortable, and then he looked directly at her to reassert his position. Doc noticed that it was the same eye formation that he himself used when looking at homeless people. But Anna O. wasn't homeless.

"You can't go."

"But I didn't even get to talk to her."

The flowers were big ones, they smelled like a really romantic date. You could bury yourself in those flowers and feel cool all over.

"Look, I can't help you," the doorman said. "Call her from the corner."

Anna ran to the corner, but Doc stayed behind until he heard the doorman mutter under his breath.

"She's pretty but she's a dyke."

But when Doc looked over at the doorman's face, he found the comment was directed at him.

Then Doc ran to the corner too. This was the Upper West Side so the pay phones worked. Anna's movements were a little wild. She wasn't really thinking about what she was doing. He could see that she was furious. She'd thought that that dress would make a difference. She was so furious in fact that Doc thought she might be rude and blow the whole thing. That's the way people lose these days. If they show how they feel it's called rude. It is called manipulation.

"Hello? Hello? Mrs. Noren? This is Anna O., Mrs. Noren. No, I am not selling you *The Watchtower*. I'm your daughter's former lover. Oh … Oh … thank you, Mrs Noren. Thank you. Thank you."

Doc followed his client into the elevator.

Chapter Seventeen

"Come in, come in," Mrs. Noren said. She had one of those huge apartments where no one lives and half the rooms are covered with drop cloths. "I'm so glad you came. How about that stinker, huh? How about that daughter of mine? What a creep."

"You know it," said Anna O.

"All the time she was telling me she did everything alone. She went on this trip alone. She went to that movie alone. She went out with this *friend*, that one. Finally I says to myself, *Helen, your daughter is a real stinker. Your daughter must be having sex with a woman. She's finally come out of the closet.* There was no other explanation. Let me tell you something, Anna, and ..."

"Doc."

"Oh, a doctor, how nice. Let me tell you that that daughter of mine is a smart girl. Too smart. She knows a lot of things that I don't know. But she only tells me things that I already know. Every word out of her mouth is one big cliché.

"Did you ever try asking her questions?" Doc suggested.

"Once," Helen answered, plopping down on a drop-cloth-covered armchair, her dress and shoes caked in plaster dust. "Once I asked her a question only because I really wanted to know the answer. It was 'Why blame communism on the Jews just because they invented it?'"

"What did she say?"

"She said, 'Ma, it's not like that anymore. Now we're as bad as anyone else, which is even more obvious.'"

"And what did you say?" Doc asked again.

"I said, 'What do you mean, "anymore"? I live here too you know, and for me it is still a current question.'"

That's when Doc took a seat because he felt so very comfortable.

"Let me tell you something Anna O.," Helen said with no sign of waning interest or energy. "Believe me, I understand you. I know why you came here. When I was young I felt the same way that you do now. The only famous person who ever looked like me was Anne Frank. Later, Ethel Rosenberg. Only martyrs for role models. You know that there's no such thing as the secret of the atom bomb? It takes thousands of volumes of information all fed into a computer. It's not like you can just add water. The Rosenbergs were executed for a crime that cannot be committed. But when will they be avenged? So, that no good kid of mine. What did she do?"

"Well ..." Anna said, sitting slowly on a dust-covered ottoman. "She used to make love to me and then roll over and say 'You're narrow because you're gay but I'm universal because I'm not.'"

"Repulsive," Helen Noren said, pulling out a box of butter cookies from under a sheet. "Oh, you brought me flowers, beautiful. Must have cost you seventeen dollars at least."

Doc ate a cookie.

"And for you, Doc, I have this book. Don't open it now. Save it for later. Here, I'll wrap it up in a paper bag and Scotch-tape the edges. Open it when you need a present."

"Thank you."

"Did you know," she said, breaking the tape with her teeth, "that a paper bag is a thing of the past? Did you notice it?"

"There are still a few stores that have them," Doc said. "Mostly stationery stores."

"Oh, really?" Helen said, handing him the package. "I never get any."

Anna O. ate a cookie.

"Honey," Helen Noren said, wrapping her arms around Anna O. and holding her close to her breast. "There is justice in this life. Don't you worry. There can be plenty of justice."

Doc listened very closely.

Later, Doc opened the package. It was a book called *Romantic Sentences*. It was blank.

Chapter Eighteen

The wind smelled clean, like clean magazines. It smelled like invisible ink. The phone rang.

"I have a collect call from Elijah Timothy Stevens. Will you accept?"

"Yes."

"Hello, uh ... is this the doctor?"

"Yes."

"I am Elijah Timothy Stevens."

"Yes?"

"I got one of your business cards the other day and I was wondering if you do phone counseling."

"If you think it would help."

"Well, Doc, it can't hurt now, can it?"

"I don't know."

"Uhm ... do you take Medicaid?"

"No. It's only ten bucks an hour."

"Well, we'll have to work out something doctor because my problem is that I am broke and ... up here in, well ... I'm in the Bastille, Doc, if you know what I mean."

"You're in jail."

"Bingo."

"Well, in that case my services are free for you, Mr. Stevens."

"Thank you, doctor. Merely accepting my collect call is halfway to a cure."

"I'm glad to hear that."

"Well, that's all I need for now, Doc. But you take care of yourself and I'll get back in touch again real soon. Don't worry. I'll be thinking about you."

"Thank you, Mr. Stevens."

"Thank you, doctor."

When he hung up the phone, he realized that the breeze through the open window was too cold, so he knew that it was one of those seasons. But he was not ready to close it. From then on there was a certain brace at the beginning of each day and a feeling in the middle of the night that he did not have enough protection.

Even turning on the radio was a flirtation with danger because certain songs could come on at any moment that would evoke memories, that would evoke specific associations that no longer needed to be considered. So, he turned it off and went back to a magazine instead. There, surprisingly, was the face that he had once known. The very face that had just been hologrammed into his mind. At first he was attracted to the grayness of the reproduction, but when he found himself unable to skim over it, he knew that there was something on that page for him. This person had won an award. She had accepted it in a white leather skirt, white patent-leather heels, and a white-see-through chiffon blouse. She was in the newspaper in that clothing. When handed her award, she said, "Thank you to all the dancers I have ever performed with for giving me the physical gratification that has kept me coming back for more."

Sometimes, thought Doc, *it is bad for people to get too much attention because their egos overinflate and they feel a certain immunity from thinking. But when a person is dismissed, it can be a blessing in disguise because then they have to be quiet and count their friends. Only then can you speak to them directly with any realistic hope of investment.*

The phone rang.

"Will you accept a collect call from Elijah Timothy Stevens?"

"Yes."

"Hi, Doc."

"Hello, Mr. Stevens. Has something happened in the last hour that you need to talk with me?"

"Yes, Doc."

"That's fine, Mr. Stevens. I just want to remind you that every patient is limited to three sessions. So this will be your second session. Understand?"

"Understood in practice, but not in theory, doctor. Why only three?"

"Mister, I'm not a martyr. I get what I need out of it by the third session and you can too. What happened?"

"Well, I used to work in a public school, a New York City public school. Do you know what that means, Doc? Can you imagine the guilt involved? It means students coming to school already disoriented instead of getting that way there the way we used to do. It means students who have never been out of their neighborhoods and don't know what *tractor* means."

"Why not?"

"Think, Doc. Think back to when we were kids. All those TV shows about farmers' daughters and talking horses. Now it's all domestic dramas. You have to watch every week in order to understand what's going on. Anyway, it means the kind of school where the principal gets busted for doing crack in the boy's john. And even worse ..."

"What could be worse than that?"

"I was that principal."

"I'm sorry, Mr. Stevens."

"They flew me up here to Ogdensburg Correctional Facility just south of the Canadian border. They flew us up on this little propeller plane called Air Rikers. They manacled our wrists together and our ankles, doctor. Then they put us on the plane. Do you think I can sell that to *The Village Voice*? I know this black girl from Yale who works up there. I want to call her and tell her about this big story but I need to charge the call somewhere. Can I charge it to you without using up my third session?"

"Yes."

"All right then, it's been good talking to you, Doc. I want you to know that I'm thinking about you and I miss you and I'll stay in touch and let you know what's going on. Okay, you be good now. Bye, Doc, love ya."

"Bye."

The phone rang.

"Will you accept a collect call from Elijah Timothy Stevens?"

"Yes."

"This is my last session, right?"

"Right."

"Okay, then I want to make sure it's a good one. I want to talk over my future."

"That's a good idea."

"Now, they've got two kinds of vocational rehabilitation training programs here. I was wondering which one you think I should take."

"What is your educational background, Mr. Stevens?"

"I have a master's in alcoholism counseling. Anyway, which program should I choose?"

"What are the possibilities?"

"Brick laying or office cleaning."

"Which one feels better to you?"

"Well, in terms of feelings, Doc, I must admit I don't feel good imagining myself behind an industrial vacuum cleaner. But I don't think that I have what it takes to commit to becoming a bricklayer. I don't think I would want to work outside with that freezing cement. So, I guess that going for practicals and not feelings, I should pick office cleaning."

"Are you comfortable with that decision?"

"No."

"What is your other option?"

"I guess I have to go back to AA, NA, get back in therapy and confront my fears."

"Are you sure?"

"Yes, I'm sure. No, I'm not sure. Yes, I'm sure."

"Well, that's our final session, Mr. Stevens. I wish you the best of luck in your life. You seem to be an open person who is really trying."

"Thank you, Doc. And, Doc, I want you to know that although we can't be together right now, I will never forget you. I think about you all the time and I don't want you to ever feel alone. I want you to know that I am thinking of you and I am someone who cares about you, Doc. I care about you. Always know that."

"I will, Mr. Stevens. Goodbye for now."

"Goodbye."

They'd both started laughing before they'd finished hanging up.

The phone rang.

"Will you accept a collect call form Elijah Timothy Stevens?"

"No," Doc said. "I just can't. It wouldn't work out."

Chapter Nineteen

All over Eastern Europe, first-time voters were electing republicans. At the same moment, here in the USA, Americans from coast to coast were jumping into taxis to go buy drugs. Communism hadn't worked out anywhere and Doc was sorry. Maybe this was the perfect time to become a Communist, when it would all be theoretical again. When it would just be about dreams.

"Hello?"

"Would you accept a collect call from Leon Stevens?"

"Yes."

"Hello, is this the doctor?"

"Yes?"

"This is Leon Stevens, Elijah Timothy's father. He told me that he was in therapy with you and I wanted to call and spill my guts too. Okay?"

"Sure."

"Well, Doc, I got two problems. One is my son and the other is a woman. Which one first?"

"That's up to you."

"Here's the thing, Doc. My son only calls me when he wants money. He never calls for anything else. I'm old now. I worked all my life and my wife is married to another man. I've got one son, Elijah Timothy Stevens. And when he calls me, it's only for money. It makes me feel bad, Doc. It makes me want to cry."

"Mr. Stevens, I have to tell you something. You son is a drug addict. That's why he calls you for money. But that doesn't mean he doesn't love you. He probably does love you. But your son is a drug addict and he needs drugs. He had to get some money so he could get drugs. But that doesn't mean he doesn't love you."

"Doctor, what is it with these drugs? I walk down the street surrounded by nodding people. Half the city is nodding."

"I noticed," Doc said.

"Can't he get in a program and get off that stuff?"

"I don't know," Doc said. "Then what would he do?"

"I don't know."

"I don't have the answer," Doc said.

"No wonder you're cheap. Tell me, Doc, do you actually help people?"

"Not really, I'm just a good listener."

"And who do you tell your thoughts to?"

"Right now, Mr. Stevens, I just don't have anything very important to say."

"Strange world, ain't it, Doc."

"Yes sir, very strange. Now, about that woman."

"Yes, that woman."

Doc leaned back in his chair and put his feet up on the table. On the radio there was nothing but racial killings, all by Italians.

"Her name was Lupita," Mr. Stevens said. "All the ways she didn't die but *aaah*, almost did. She ate that fruit. The fan crashed down onto the bed. Lupe rolled over but the minister was mangled. Then there was that crazy kid with the stick."

"Go on."

"One day, eating her corn chips with painted nails, Lupita says, 'You are the fifteenth person in my life to whom I've said "You're fucking me so good. How can anyone fuck me so good?"' Doc, it changes you to realize things like that."

"Brings it all down to scale," Doc said.

"Her greatest moment, her shining youth. They all applauded at the Mexican Opera. They cheered when she sang 'My Way.' They were all there – Jorge, Hector, Hank (the secretary of tourism), the three Trotskyites in a pickup truck. She wore a red dress, of course."

"Is she involved with someone else?"

"Her boyfriend's name is Raoul. She lives upstairs on Avenue B. She only takes medication. She went to the bodega in her bathrobe. She buys vitamins over the phone. She had one great night. At the opera. The opera."

It flashed, in Doc's mind, that this could be the same woman Anna O. had mentioned in her list of past lovers. He almost asked, "Is she insatiably multiorgasmic?" But he decided it would be tacky. Therapists are supposed to have blank slates, not coincidences.

"Mr. Stevens," said Doc, barely overcome, "that was so poetic. You must have loved her very much."

"Well, Doc, sometimes I'm obsessed with my love for her. And then again, sometimes I tell myself that there is no need to take desire and dress it up as beauty."

"Why not?" Doc asked.

"You mean it's okay?"

"Sure. Desire and beauty? What's the difference anyway?"

"Don't know. Anyway, later I looked back and discovered that my moments with Lupe Colón were really the best. I remembered how good they felt and how much I enjoyed them."

"That's wonderful, Mr. Stevens. I envy you there."

"But Doctor, I didn't think you were allowed to make statements like that. I'm the patient. I thought you were supposed to be a blank slate."

That blank slate again.

"Well, Mr. Stevens, my theory of therapy is based on the belief that we may as well tell everything we know. So, what happened, Mr. S? What happened to you and Lupe Colón?"

"This is the sad part, Doc. The part that haunts me. One night, I was lying in her bed while she was walking around the apartment naked, looking at her own body in the mirror. I reached under some pillows to prop up my head and pulled out a long, thin rod. I held it round in my hand for a minute trying to imagine what it could possibly be doing there. Then I realized that this woman was jacking off with an iron rod. She was two-timing me with a pipe. A pipe! I knew that girl was tough but I didn't like the idea of her sitting on machinery when I was home with my wife. So I started looking around the apartment – snooping, you know. And there was metal everywhere. Everywhere. I'd been so blind. All the evidence was sitting right under my nose but I never put two and two together. She had metal radiators, silverware, window gates, a file cabinet, and she was using them all for sex. For sex! Doctor, this was fifteen years ago and it still haunts me at night. I can't help but imagining, over and over again, Lupita in bed with a muffin tray, tweezers, an iron. It makes me sick. I suffer every night. Doctor, I can't sleep."

"Mr. Stevens," Doc said, "did it ever occur to you that the iron rod might have been a weapon? It might be a weapon?"

"A weapon?"

"Many women sleep with weapons. Did you know that, Mr. Stevens?"

"No, Doc, I did not."

"Well, it's true."

"You mean she wasn't cheating on me with a tube?"

"Possibly not."

"She was so beautiful that night, Doc."

"Which night?"

"At the opera, the opera."

Chapter Twenty

Doc's mind was opening irreversibly like a banana or a can of Tab. He was realizing, quite specifically, that all over the world people are looking for and comparing themselves to others who don't exist. It's the international invisible.

We are each other's worst fears, humanized, he thought.

This placed him solidly in relation to everyone else and, therefore, the universe. Badly, but superbly, he imagined comets, planets, satellites, asteroids, space stations, and telecommunications technology still unknowable from the street.

Doc had recently been contacted by a new set of clients, a couple that were having problems loving each other. He saw their arrival as a wonderful opportunity to try out his new perspective on people giving themselves and each other a break.

Of course this reminded him of his own experiences with that woman. Then it occurred to Doc that everything fit together. All along he had believed, instinctually, that his broken heart had something to do with the collapse of the culture. He had wanted to blame it on economics instead of on the fact that she was a fucking bitch.

Eureka, I found it, Doc thought, so gleefully. *I've solved my own and other people's problems.*

Doc needed to get his shit together. That couple was coming in a few days. What exactly did he have to offer them? In preparation, Doc reviewed what he already knew about fighting couples. Usually, Doc observed, one of the members was destroying with more rapidity than the other. These types of situations are very difficult for the therapist, because long ago a propaganda evolved claiming that they could not exist. "It takes two to tango" isn't even true on the dance floor. One person can do a lot of evil all on his or her own. But the Theory of Mutual Blame arose sometime before Doc was even born. Perhaps it was a takeoff on Freud's seduction theory or the more generic practice of blaming victims for being alive. Its origins were unclear, but no one had ever had to take full responsibility for their own actions since.

Doc relaxed. If he could only get that woman in the white leather to stop interrupting and be kind instead, all America would change. She would have to think about things and America would have to too. All his life Doc had been told that America was the freest country on earth. America is the most powerful country on earth. We're number one. We're number one. And Americans believed it because, after all, what did they know? To the north there was nothing and to the south there were people who wanted their jobs. All they could look in the eye was each other. It was just like that woman in white leather.

One day Doc and she were walking around Manhattan. It was a cool day, crisp, one of those days where the buildings stand out in the sunlight, shining like a razor. Doc was filled with love. He turned to her, the leather cap white, like the clouds, and said, "Isn't it exciting that now that we're both finishing up big projects, the whole world is open before us and anything can happen?"

But she, she acted just like America. She said, "Don't compare yourself to me."

They both think they're so great but there's not one ounce of truth in the whole shebang. The country is so big now anyway no one can know what's really going on in there. No one's got a grip on it. The TV is run by God. What do all those blondes have to do with us? The newspapers have football on the front page. The only thing Doc knew for sure about the United States of America was that virtually everyone in it used to smoke pot.

When the phone rang this time he glanced at the magazine

beckoning from the corner but got distracted by the silence on the other end. The person was still there but they would not talk. Doc felt a twisted excitement.

"Hello?" Doc said. "Hello? Hello? Hello? Hello?"

He recognized the tactic and wanted power because he was so afraid of the person attached to it.

"Hello?" he said, wanting to keep it going as long as possible. "Hello? *Hello?*" as though he had never said it before because he was unwilling to let on that he had. If she would just answer he would let it all go.

When he hung up Doc had an emotional reaction, the kind that is hypnotizing. He was trapped in a brick. He was the subject of a million stories. He went to the other side of the street. He was too far from the racetrack. He had egg on his hands.

It was quiet. Doc sat in his chair. Outside there were people in the street trying to murder one another. Doc listened carefully. None of them were his clients. Once he'd stopped paying attention there was an illusion of silence. Finally other lives and their murmuring had ceased to penetrate. Doc fell asleep.

Four hours later, he awoke resolving to give more to his clients.

Doc had an appointment coming up with the couple, and this time he really wanted to make a difference. So he decided to take the dramatic step of consulting with his mentor, the elderly Herr K.

Chapter Twenty-One

Herr Doktor K. came shuffling down the block. His hair was purely white. His beard was purely white. His skin was translucent. His eyes were blue. His glasses were as thick as the bottoms of Coke bottles. He wore a black suit with vest and fedora. He carried a well-worn mahogany cane.

"Doktor," said Doc. "Thank you for meeting with me. I hope I find you in the best of health."

"Ya vell, doctor," said Herr Doktor K., "I am, I'm afraid, a victim of the mental health system. I have spent the last thirty years of my life caring for the most desperate and disturbed people of New York City, six days a week. Rarely do I have the chance to discuss with someone who is in control of their own behavior. Even since the budget cuts, psychiatric patients must wait three days before we can find them a bed. I spend ten hours a day with people who are handcuffed to chairs, attempted suicides before the age of twelve, patricide, matricide, infanticide, genocide, homicide, fratricide."

"What do they call it if you kill your sister?"

"Tsuriscide. That's a joke."

"Herr K., what a toll this must take on your life."

"You shouldn't know from it. I can't hear. I can't see. I can't walk. I can't remember."

"How old are you now, Herr K.?"

"Forty-eight."

They took seats in the window of Café Geiger on East Eighty-sixth Street. The Doktor ordered Sascher Torte mit Schlag and

Koffee. The Doctor ordered Jell-O and Sanka.

"Look around you," whispered Herr K. "The greatest talents in the study of the human mind. Look, Doktor Frankfurter of Frankfurt, the one with his teeth on the tablecloth. He discovered Valium. And he's not even smiling. All dat money he made, the poor schlep never even took a vacation. And in the corner, Doktor Helena Schwartz Von Klingenfelder, discoverer of sibling rivalry."

"How does she get along with hers?"

"They were all killed in concentration camps."

K. wiped his glasses on his shirt.

"Doktor Schwartz Von Klingenfelder and Doktor Frankfurter from Frankfurt had a love affair in 1932 and they still won't speak to each other. It's a strange group, these German Jews. They produced Marx, Freud, Einstein, Hannah Arendt, and Walter Benjamin. Look at them now. They can't even chew."

Doktor K. was the Doc's mentor. He had been a pioneer in the field of interruption theory and the world's most renowned expert on the patterns some people enforce in order to keep others from finishing their sentence.

"Herr K., I come to you seeking your esteemed advice on a very interesting case."

"Doctor," said the Doktor. "I am happy for you that you have an interesting case. Knowing how to observe is not enough. You still need something meaningful to look at."

Then he fell to his knees and began to have convulsions.

As Doc watched him writhe on the floor he noticed what a symbol K. was of another time.

"Better now?" Doc asked.

"Ya, ya, gut, gut," Doktor answered, brushing himself off and only drooling slightly. "Are you still there?"

"Oh yeah," Doc answered. "I didn't go anywhere and I haven't come back."

Herr K.'s neck looked like hand-carved wood, peeled and ribbed, rubbed raw and pink.

"Now that I'm reaching old age, I watch myself very carefully," K. said, wiping his glasses on a linen handkerchief.

"What do you see?"

"I see that after a lifetime of analyzing, I do it instinctively even when there is nothing worth understanding."

"I've noticed the same pattern in myself," Doc answered.

Doc then relayed the case of his couple who would not decide to listen. As Doc spoke, Herr K. ate his Schlag, every once in a while pausing to cough up phlegm. It was an uncontrollable condition that did not disgust Doc. In fact, he found it endearing, like the way one gets used to a lover's growing deafness. Whenever the tone gets too low, you lean over automatically, waiting for her to say, "What?"

"Doctor," said K. "Listen to me closely and you will understand."

"I know," Doc said.

"There are words like *emotions*, which I will refer to here as *chemical reactions*. Now, we know that there is a part of the brain that is responsible for feelings such as anger, fear, tenderness. Then there is a part of the brain that is concerned with perception, awareness, comprehension, understanding. They are connected."

"Spiritually?"

"No, biologically," K. continued. "Certain experiences, for example, abandonment, create chemical reactions that disrupt these connections and result in keeping awareness away from emotions, psychologically. Denial is actually a chemical condition. People in this state protect themselves from information that they are not equipped to handle. Then they remain psychologically unaware of their own feelings. To keep this information out permanently requires large amounts of interruption."

"Oh," said Doc. "I never thought of it that way."

"Now," Herr K. said. "This may appear to you to be a crackpot theory. But, frankly, doctor, what isn't? If you think there is one true explanation for anything, you are wrong. So, understanding that, my explanation is as good as any."

Doc whacked his package of Sanka against the table before tearing it open. But the water was tepid and the granules lay there in brown clumps.

"But, Doktor, if your theory is true, then the only people who can understand the human mind are scientists. Second, what about responsibility? Isn't listening a human responsibility and aren't people responsible for their own behavior despite all the excuses our culture has invented?"

"Doctor," said the Doktor. "Politically and morally, I agree. But politics and morality have little to do with human functioning. The sad reality is that people do not listen and do not take responsibility. A lifetime in the office and in the laboratory have not revealed a way to change all that. In conclusion, doctor, there are many people who will be civil to someone who is extraordinarily kind. There are very few who will be kind first. If you want to call this a lack of responsibility then, I'm afraid, doctor, that you will be a more unhappy man than I who call it simply a series of chemical reactions."

Chapter Twenty-two

Two weeks had passed and Anna had felt no need to telephone Doc. Besides, her three sessions were over. She knew what the relationship would be when she stepped into it. And now it was done. Mrs. Noren's love had thrown Anna a bit off course. It was like she had forgotten about that side of life. She needed some time to just sit around. She needed time to put her feelings in order.

"Phrase it, I mean, face it," Anna said.

She was thinking about sounds when the telephone rang. She let it ring and then thought about words. There were only words for a limited number of feelings. This became increasingly inadequate, inappropriate, inaccurate. Anna named a few ideas for which she needed words.

– Stop talking so you can be happy.
– Saying something prejudiced and later insisting it wasn't.
– I only have power when I destroy.
– That place between the shoulder and the breast.

The phone rang again.

Anna had been feeling suspicious all afternoon because she was contemplating how to get ahead in a dying civilization. The options for growth industry seemed to be HIV counseling, hospice work, or teaching English to Russians. This fed into an ongoing suspicion she'd been having about her telephone ever since tiny beeps started to appear during the course of banal conversations. Only she could hear them. The other person could never hear them. Finally she decided that her phone was being tapped. It was a natural conclusion for someone of her generation. They expect the government to oppress them. As she would speak and listen to the beeps, she would listen to herself more carefully to try and determine what it was the government was after. But that never became clear.

Anna noticed a pattern evolving as a result of her therapy. Maybe people offered more than she had ever known and the government offered less.

When the phone stopped ringing she perceived a peculiar silence. One of many. Which one? There is a silence of perception. It wasn't that. Thoughtless silence? Forced silence? Chosen silence? Silence because you're listening. Fearful silence. Because the radio's broken. Hesitation. When you don't say it because you don't want to hurt the other person. Enraged silence. When you don't say it because it's not going to do any good. Waiting. Thinking. Not wanting to be misunderstood. Refusing to participate. Self-absorption. When a loud sound is over. Shame.

The phone started ringing again. She let it.

Chapter Twenty-three

The next day the phone rang and there was silence again. Doc wanted to sound loving. He knew it would give him more power. He wanted to sound like someone that this person would want to be kind to. But he couldn't think fast enough, so he said something weird instead.

"I know you're reaching out," he said. "I know you're doing the best you can. I'll hang up now and turn on the machine so you can leave a message."

Only, somehow, saying the words "leave a message" sounded awfully flat. It had become impossible to include them in casual language without sounding robotic. She didn't call back.

"So, John," Doc said as he and Cro-Mag wrapped up their final session. "I'd like you to tell me about your artwork. You refer to it regularly but you never say exactly what it is that you do."

"My art is like ... jazz ... man."

"In what way?"

"Well, it comes out of the body."

"The body?"

"Well, my body. In other words, I'm the one who makes it."

"But what is it about?"

"It's about intentionally undermining meaning."

"Would you say that it's about being?"

Doc intentionally opened the window.

"No ... it's too ethereal to be summed up."

"Well, I don't mean to ask you to reduce your art, but could you tell me what values are at its core?"

"Doc, my work is based in values by chance."

"You mean it's about nothing."

"Well, there are some materials."

"Which ones?"

"Time and space. Sequence and duration. You know, lack and all that stuff. Naked brain."

"*Naked brain*?" said Doc. "Now that's interesting. How did you think of that?

"I saw it on TV when I was stoned."

"Do you watch a lot of TV?"

"I don't know."

"What do you like about TV?"

"It's so colorfully constructed along the lines of color."

"Oh, you have a color TV?"

"Yeah, a really cheap one. A lousy one. A broken-down one. I don't have enough money for anything decent."

"John, let me ask you a difficult question."

"Huh?"

"Why do you think that you are poor? What in the world gives you that impression?"

"Doc, the above is equal to the below, so I am as proletarian as the next guy."

"Frankly that sounds like peripheral logic to me."

"*Peripheral logic*? Wow, Doc, now you've got a good one. What channel?"

"Uh, I don't have a TV."

"So, I'm subletting my apartment – at profit, of course – and going on vacation for a while."

"Again? Where to?"

"Well, my family has an estate in Georgia. I like to go down there."

"What kinds of things do you do down there?"

"Oh, you know, going to the dentist, supervising the plantation, fucking slaves."

Okay, Doc thought. *This is my chance. I have a prime example of the oppressor class right here in my living room/office. Someone who knows absolutely nothing about how other people are living, someone who defines the world uniquely by his own experience and is a parasitic complainer. I have to use every element of my analytic ability to find a way to explain to Cro-Mag why that is not an acceptable way of thinking. I have to explain why that way of thinking is a product of, and at the same time a prototype for, a very sick way of life. If I try hard enough and am logical enough and am clear enough, I will be able to save all the people who will have to come into contact with this shmuck.*

"You racist maggot," Doc said.

"What's your problem, Doc, can't you take a joke?"

It can't be, Doc thought. *It just can't be. If Herr K. is right then there is no point to therapy. If you can't help people be responsible and kind then why be with them at all. Why interact*?

Doc had to face the truth, that he was old-fashioned. He was always looking for a simple, familiar, low-tech solution. But people are no longer interested in analysis. They all prefer catharsis now. They all prefer to say that they are helpless and can't change other people, i.e. the world. Marxism has been replaced by postmodernism. Psychoanalysis has been replaced by twelve-step programs. It was the end of the content. The whole way of looking at things was changing, and Doc was left behind.

Chapter Twenty-four

The next afternoon, Doc sat on the chair in the middle of his apartment. In the refrigerator were frozen carrots, a pink doughnut, leftover carryout waffles, grape soda, and orange soda. It was beautiful. It was also sometime in the afternoon and all the light came from outside, in puddles, which changes things. As time passed, the light moved to different spots and got smaller or longer or other variations on shape. There was no thought as pleasant to Doc as sleep.

If only I could perfect forgetting and being awake at the same time, Doc thought, *I'd be happy and put the alcohol and pharmaceutical companies out of business simultaneously.*

The doorbell rang. They were here.

Remember, Doc told himself, *lovers can be happy together. Just be nice to each other and let the other one know that you like them. You don't have to say "I like you" morning, noon, and night. But show it by being caring and compassionate toward them. And let them finish their sentences.*

Doc was excited now.

"I will show Herr Doktor K. that he is wrong," Doc swore. "I will show the world how very much people can do."

The doorbell rang again. Doc took his place.

"Break a leg," he told himself before the lights came up. No more heartbreak for these two. This time Doc would not let them down. This play was called

FAILURE

As the lights come up JO *and* SAM *are kissing. Then they separate and stand apart.*

DOC

So, how are you two feeling today?

JO

Doc, I'm so happy today. I was just thinking about how, now that we're both coming here and trying to work on our relationship, it is so exciting because anything can happen.

SAM

Don't compare yourself to me. I'm older than you. I've been in this world a lot longer than you have. You're always trying to make me be just like you. Well, I'm never going to be just like you. You can't take it. You're threatened. You're threatened because you're narrow. But I'm universal. That's why I'm marginalized. Because I'm transcendent.

That phrase – *don't compare yourself to me* – it was exactly what the woman in white leather had said to Doc. The logical and psychological interpretation would be that that woman and Sam felt *inferior* and so pretended that they were more. But Doc wanted to hear it straight from the patient's mouth.

DOC

Excuse me, Sam. I'm sorry to interrupt your therapy like this, but that phrase, that word *compare*. Why did you say that? Was it on TV or something? Is that a new "in" insult or something?

JO

Stop lecturing me about how terrible I am.

Shit, thought Doc. *Now Jo had to go stick in his two cents just when I was about to get an answer. Now Sam has free reign to react and he won't have to answer anything at all.*

SAM

Don't tell me who I am. Don't tell me what I'm doing. You don't know me. You don't know anything about me. You think you know everything but you know nothing. You're a hundred percent wrong, a hundred percent wrong, a hundred percent wrong, a hundred percent wrong. You're a hundred percent wrong, a hundred percent wrong. You're a hundred percent wrong, you're wrong, you're wrong, you're wrong, you're wrong, you're wrong, you're a hundred percent wrong. You're a hundred percent wrong. You're a hundred percent wrong, a hundred percent wrong. You're a hundred percent wrong, a hundred percent wrong. You're a hundred percent wrong, a hundred percent wrong. You're a hundred percent wrong, a hundred percent wrong. You're wrong. You're wrong. You're a hundred percent wrong. Wrong, wrong, wrong, wrong, wrong, wrong, wrong, wrong, wrong. You're wrong, wrong, wrong, wrong, wrong, wrong, wrong, wrong. You're a hundred percent wrong, a hundred percent wrong, a hundred percent wrong, a hundred percent wrong. You're wrong, wrong. You're wrong, wrong. You're wrong, wrong, wrong, wrong. You're a hundred percent wrong. Wrong, wrong a hundred percent wrong. A hundred percent wrong. A hundred percent wrong. You're wrong, wrong, wrong, wrong, wrong, wrong, wrong.

BLACKOUT

"*Stop!*" Doc said. "*Wait!*"

"*You!*" he said, pointing at Sam. "What did you get out of that?"

"You're wrong," Sam said.

"What did you get?" Doc asked, pointing to Jo.

"I wasn't listened to," Jo said.

"Okay!" Doc said. "Okay, if you would only become aware of your behavior, you could change it. People don't want to be awful. But they do want to repeat the same old stuff and incidentally have it all work out. Now you, Jo, and you, Sam, your brain chemicals aren't in control. You are. You are. You are!"

"Well, Doc," Jo said, "I can offer one thing."

"What?"

"When Sam puts me down, I can't listen precisely. It's too hurtful."

"Sam," Doc said, really excited, "we're finally getting somewhere here. It's wonderful. We're inching toward a breakthrough. See, Sam? See, Sam? Jo is making you an offering. Sam, answer this question. What is more important to you? Would you rather put Jo down or be listened to?"

"I don't put Jo down," Sam said. "But Jo is too threatened to realize that."

"Why is Jo threatened?"

"Because Jo cannot compare Jo to me."

Doc placed his head in his hands and wept.

Chapter Twenty-five

"I'm wrong. I'm a hundred percent wrong," said Doc, hours and hours after the couple was long gone. "I'm wrong. I'm wrong. I'm a hundred percent wrong."

Meanwhile, back at her place, Anna was reading through a stack of old *People* magazines. The covers were really shiny. They glistened.

TODAY'S LATEST FLAP: NOW IT'S JANE IN THE HOT SEAT

This is why she was going crazy. Why was *Today* italicized? How could *Today* be a euphemism? Especially one expected to be so easily understood that it could appear on a national magazine without any explanation? Then it occurred to her that *Today* was a product of some kind, or a packaged event and not these twenty-four hours.

Doc looked up at the empty apartment.

"I, like others, have been hurt," Doc said. "I needed to be treated kindly and with love and instead I was interrupted. I looked around outside my door and noticed that virtually nothing in this society gets thought through or completely said. So, I decided to do something about it. I decided to work for change on a one-to-one basis. I took direct action on behalf of listening and nothing happened."

Anna grabbed another magazine.

BUILT FOR THE HUMAN RACE, said that week's ad from Nissan. Then there was an advertisement for a Rabbit Ovulation Computer.

It was for that special sector of the population that could no longer easily conceive and not the group that was plagued by the epidemic of unwanted pregnancies, both teenage and adult. The advertisement was a full page but designed to look smaller. It pretended that it did not want to attract your attention. It was designed to ensure that the reader's infertility would remain a secret. It was black and white so no one would know.

Doc, on the other hand, sat there complacently for hours. At some point he became aware that there was a shooting going on outside. It was like any other shooting. The guns go off. There's a moment of silence. People start to scream. Horns start to honk as the screaming and then voyeuring public start to block traffic. Then the sirens come.

Another gun went off.

Oh well, someone else got popped, Doc thought.

Then he realized that there was a continuous knocking at his front door but he did not react. Instead, Doc sat in the vortex of three windows, each reaching out with a vector of light. The spot where they met was called *him* and was the warmest spot of all. The edges quivered surprisingly because the heart of that point seemed so solid and dependable. But there was some hint of potential erosion, some natural disaster.

Is that what you'd call a description? he thought.

Anna turned to the record section. There were some really strange reviews. One said, "The 'Nuke the Baby Whales' crowd would oppose many of his positions."

What in the world is the "Nuke the Baby Whales crowd"? Anna wondered. Then she read another record review on the same page. "Delighted depravity of drug-afflicted and/or homosexual incidents. Pervo-novelty songs."

I wonder who would buy that record as a result of this review?

The next record was described as "as heartfelt as anything since Janis Joplin."

Is that a pick or a pan? Anna wondered.

The knocking continued.

If that person really wants to get in, they will. I'm in no condition to do anything precise about that right now.

One minute into the book section and Anna noticed that every book had the same name, *Nintendo Power, Nintendo Strategies, How to Win at Nintendo, Captain Nintendo.*

Anna could not tell what Nintendo was from the titles, even when she really tried. It seemed like some new kind of generic activity. But she could not get closer than that.

The door finally opened.

"Anna," the stranger said. "Anna, I've come to speak with you."

Doc looked over his shoulder for Anna but he was the only other person in the room. Then he looked back in the intruder's direction. Doc recognized her voice the way he recognized machine sounds. That's when the panic began to set in. That voice had surrounded him every day like the sound of a prewar elevator. Like the refrigerator buzz after the electricity had been turned on. Like that particularly loose floorboard that means *your* house. Like books always falling in the other room, it was engraved on his gray matter. Suddenly it became obvious how many feelings Doc had left out because they were all contained in that other person's voice. The air between them was a membrane. She spoke like the neighbors watching TV. The neighbors getting plastered. The neighbors falling down on the other side of the Sheetrock.

"Anna?" she asked again.

When she stepped into his line of vision he got smacked by the gestures. Especially by the fact that she had acquired new ones and no longer moved exactly as his mind had recorded her gestures' greatest hits. She was shorter than he remembered. His memory had not been short because it took place at the top of his head, slightly above eye level. She was wearing her usual outfit, that white-leather-and-chiffon dance thing.

"Anna," she said. "I've come to speak to you."

Then she sat down on the couch and took out the cigarette.

"Six months after you left me, Anna, I was still in love with you. After nine months, while fucking someone else on a regular basis, I was still in love with you. Now, after a year with that guy, I have to get you back in my life. I have to because my life is less pleasurable without you in it."

Doc saw a hole in her stocking. It seemed to be there on purpose.

"Anna, why are you dressed like a man?"

Doc looked at her in disbelief. Why was she being so kind? Had she undergone that cathartic trauma that was the only possible mode of transformation into a nice person?

"How did you find me?"

"Don't give me that bullshit," she said.

So he knew that nothing had changed.

"Don't give me that bullshit. You go traipsing all the way up to my mother's house with some sob story, leave messages on my phone machine about your fucking birthday, read about me in the newspapers and then make it sound like that's my fault too. Like it's all me. All me. Me me me me me me me. All me. All me. Me me me all me all me."

"You," he said, slowly awakening. "Time and time again you chose your rage over me."

"Every time I was in the newspaper," she said. "I knew you were reading it. I couldn't have any privacy from you. It drove me crazy. Even in my glory you never left me alone."

When she exhaled her smoke, it smelled so good. It was instantly calming and intimate.

"Anna," the woman said. "Please have some faith. I'm sorry I wasn't good to you. I'm sorry I didn't help you. But I've been working on myself. I've been working toward a place of compassionate awareness."

"Is that a new therapy movement?" Doc asked.

"No, Anna, it's my own personal goal. Why are you dressed as a man?

Doc slid off the chair and onto the floor. Then he squatted. Then he touched the floor to the top of his head. Then he climbed back onto the chair and waited.

"Why are you dressed like a man?"

"I wanted the sympathy."

"Listen, Anna," she said. "In this entire event of you and me there is only one word that has no meaning and that word is *he*. Why do you use it? Are you trying to be absurd?"

"I use *he*," said Doc, "because it's easier and I need all the help I can get."

"Huh?"

"Let's say," he continued, "let's say that a man has a job at a fancy newspaper. He gets up in the morning and all his clothes are wrinkled, but instead of ironing them, he takes the least wrinkled shirt and wears it to work. When he gets there, a message is waiting that his girlfriend tried to commit suicide for the third time. He heads toward the hospital but stops off at a bar where he gets drunk, meets a woman, and goes home with her for sex. Now, how do you feel about his man?"

"Well," she said, "he's not a saint. But if that's his girl's third try, then she's got some problem of her own beyond his control."

"Okay," Doc said, getting really exhausted. "Now, what if we took exactly the same scenario but with a woman. A woman has a job at a fancy newspaper. Okay, already she's either a frigid workaholic, slept her way to the top, or is an affirmative action hire. She gets up in the morning and all her clothes are wrinkled. How could that be unless she'd stayed up all night downing a pitcher of martinis, fucking the boss, or working till the sun rose, thanks to her addiction to diet pills. We haven't even considered the ironing board yet and already she's a candidate for *Beyond the Valley of the Dolls*. If she actually showed up at the office in a wrinkled blouse, we would have to spend the rest of the book justifying it. Now do you understand why I use *he*?"

"But Anna, what does that have to do with you being a lesbian?"

The sky was dead blue. A pool of chestnut, like a bruise.

What had white leather done to think she deserved such a confidence?

"I'm not trying to pass," Doc said. "Except to myself. I mean, how many times can a person be told in a multitude of ways that she will never be fully human because she is not a man? The logical conclusion is to become a man to herself, simply to retain the most basic self-respect."

The woman stood there smoking. She didn't say anything abusive so Doc took that as an encouraging sign.

"Since I was a child," he said, "there have been two epithets that I have truly feared. I feared being told 'You want to be a man,' and I feared being told 'You hate men.' I feared them because they were spoken with such insidious innuendo by so many different kinds of people. And each time the most obvious message was that the man in that sentence was more important than me."

Doc took a deep breath.

"I feared those accusations so much that I did everything I could to prove them both wrong. But it was like trying to avoid both sides of the coin. It was like being accused of belonging to the Jewish-Bolshevik-bankers' conspiracy. I was trying to prove that I was not something that could actually never exist. It was like the secret of the atom bomb. Freud says I was *driven into homosexuality* because I wanted to have my father's child. The end result was that I, Anna

O., could not exist. I was nothing. I only existed relationally. I only existed in relation to men. I'm sick of being a reflection. How many times do I have to come out? And do I always have to do it anecdotally? When it's not a story, but a constant clash of systems. When it's a traveling implosion?"

Doc looked closely at the woman in white, waiting for her to reply.

"You," she said. "You're obsessed by your homosexuality."

"What about yours?" Doc said.

"That's why you left me," the woman answered, bitterly. "Because I wasn't a big enough *dyke*."

Things were moving too fast for Doc. He didn't have time to observe. The only choice seemed to be to get involved or go comatose. He knew his name was Anna, but he didn't really feel like a woman yet. He still wanted so badly to exist.

"No, I left you because you don't listen," Doc said. "But you weren't listening when I told you that, so you'll never ever know."

"Forget it, Anna," the woman screamed. "Don't tell me what to do. Don't tell me how to act. The next thing you know you'll be comparing yourself to me and trying to force me to invite you to my mother's house for Christmas."

That was just the beginning. She was yelling and yelling. Watching her screams made this woman into an object. There had been a time, now past, when this woman's body had been a very close thing, sometimes as close as Doc's own body. Or at least as close as his wrists. Slender, fashionable, or anything that denoted shape, ceased. What Doc saw instead was the meeting of two fleshy thighs that could be parted. Or, the indentation left by elastic. He'd hear a word repeated mercilessly accompanied by a merciless gesture. It was that breakdown into sections that familiarity brings. He was being called Anna but he did not feel like Anna.

I've sometimes had sex with my worst enemies, Doc flashed. *Because it was the only way to defeat them. If I have sex with them, then – for that moment – I am important in their lives. They need me to get off. It's a triumph, being important.*

"Uhh," he said.

"Are you saying that as a man or a woman?" she asked spitefully.

"What difference does it make?" Doc sputtered. "As long as I mean it the same either way."

"You can't mean it the same either way," the woman answered. "Believe me. I'm a woman all the time and I know."

Doc started to cry.

"What are you going to do now, Anna, cry in my ear? Crying is a manipulation. Saying how you feel is a manipulation because it gives information with the hopes of impacting on my behavior. Get it? Get it?"

Dock took out a gun and shot her.

Then the doorbell rang.

"Who's there?"

"It's me."

Oh no, Doc thought. *It's Cro-Mag.*

"What do you want?" Doc yelled through the door.

"Doc?" he said. "I figured it all out. I figured out the answer to my problem. I found a way to understand the world."

Despite being covered in blood, Doc could not resist a good solution so he cracked the front door slightly and peeked out from under the chain.

"Yes?"

"Well," Cro-Mag said. "I don't have to be guilty anymore. That way no one will ever ask me embarrassing questions again."

Now what am I going to do? Doc thought.

Chapter Twenty-six

Chapter twenty-five is a lie. At least, the end of it is. That is not what happened. That was just Doc projecting his worst fears onto the page. Actually he and this woman stepped out for a cup of coffee.

"There's an Algerian Marxist with a falafel stand on Ninth Street," Doc said. "There are two Palestinian brothers running a deli on Tenth. Across the street from them is the mosque and around the corner is the Halal butcher. There are worshipers standing around all the time. The Arabs stand together. The Pakistanis stand together. Each speaks and stands a different way. When I step into Di Robertis Italian Coffee Shop for a Sanka and an éclair, there are always a variety of Muslims standing in line with white caps buying coffee.

"And down here, on the other corner, is Babu who sells *New York Posts* and *People* magazines from his newsstand. He has a PhD in political science from the University of Delhi and has a hard time meeting American intellectuals."

Doc had so many things he wanted to tell her.

Doc felt good walking next to this mean woman. There was something great about it.

"What do you like about me, Anna?" the woman finally asked.

"I like the way you like flowers," Doc said. "I like your muscles. I like the way you kiss when you come." Then Doc added, "I haven't been myself lately."

"Why, because you've been alone?"

"No," Doc answered, "because I've been without you."

They never spoke to each other again.

Chapter Twenty-seven

Is it because of windows that I think
the day's square?
– Eileen Myles

Finally, the inevitable happened. Doc met a woman on the subway. Her name was Dora. She listened quietly while Doc told her everything.

"You don't look like a man to me," Dora said. "You don't smell like one, you don't feel like one or act like one."

"Okay," Doc said, trying to relax and trying on the label *Anna* at the same time. "Okay, but that woman in white really made me feel like one of the guys."

"Well," Dora answered, "obviously you couldn't give her what she needed."

"What was that?"

"She needed you to prove that she is heterosexual."

That resonated so thoroughly with Anna. She felt so suddenly at ease.

"Where are you from?" Anna asked.

"Oh, a small town in Pennsylvania," Dora answered. "And then the Bronx."

"Finally," Anna said, "do you have any idea of how long I have been waiting for you?"

Anna O. had been out in public and had seen Dora some time before. Later, as they were fucking, Dora made little sounds, said little words here and there that Anna could play back later.

"How could you possibly think you were a man?" Dora said. "When you have such a big, hungry pussy."

Anna was fast while Dora was slow and sharp. It took her forever to get ready. Once in bed, Anna came on strong and was rough. But Dora really knew how to make love. They were gorgeous girls with lips of glass until they kissed. Then their fucking was a carefree heedless motion. It was emotionally connected. It made them want to be friends for a long, long time.

"I'm good at service but bad at surrender," Anna confided.

"Just left your skirt over your head," Dora said, whispering to her the way shadows fall.

"I forgot I was a woman," Anna said, following orders.

"Don't do it again," Dora said. "You don't have to."

"I feel a little crazy," Anna said. "Look, goose bumps."

"You don't have to compete with men when you're here with me. I want *you*, honey."

It was different this time. It had gone beyond anything fleshy. It was carnal desire both ways but Dora liked to speak directly of love and Anna only let it spill out.

It was one of those rare moments where temptation and joy were the same things. They were lucky, these two. Touching each other was right.

Now Anna had everything. She was a woman again. She did not have to be Doc. She could be loved instead. She learned that what she had been taught about right and wrong was created for a world that no longer existed and actually never did exist. She learned that a person positions herself on quicksand. She learned that every single individual has to rethink morality for themselves and at the same time come to a newly negotiated social agreement. That's how Anna learned to be many people at once and live in different worlds of perception at the same time each day.

She lived in the world where she was a man. She lived in the world where she was a woman. She lived in the world with an unresolvable past and a world with a resolvable future. She lived in the world that could be explained and in the one that could not.

At night one woke to touch the other. She responded by turning. Gray light. Light blue. Her bones turned underneath. Even her shifts were tender. Simple words are the best.

Anna looked at herself in the mirror. She was attentive and flirtatious; the room smelled of whiskey, blood, and sex.

"Dora, tell me a story while I admire you. Tell me about the first time you fell in love."

Dora was lying back, neatly, on the pillow. Her lips were relaxed so she looked like herself as a young girl.

"The first time? It's been a while since someone has asked me that. Let's see, it was back in Lancaster, PA, when I was seventeen. My first real girlfriend was named Pauline Greene. I was working on Broad Street before the mall – selling, like what I do now. And she used to come by on her motorbike claiming to be shopping for nylons. I didn't have a boyfriend. I just didn't want that. And she kept hanging around pretending she was looking at the hosiery but she was really looking at me. Finally she asked me out on a formal date. I remember I was so nervous. I was wearing a white blouse and no bra. We drove around and listened to the radio and talked until she parked the car so we could make out. It was so exciting. I had my arms around this strong woman who wanted me and it was so exciting. We stayed together in that house for five years. Everybody knew about it but I didn't say anything so they didn't say anything either. Then she left me."

"Were you surprised?"

"One day I was all curled up next to her and then she wasn't in my life anymore. But all around were these ... remnants. I would find strands of her hair on the sheets. Her fingerprints were on the glasses. I couldn't do anything but wait until it all disappeared. And it did. The day I realized that everything was gone I cried so hard I couldn't believe I was actually alive. But you have to work. I was alone for a long time after that. Then I moved to New York."

"What happened next?"

"I changed completely," Dora said. "I look back on my own life story now and I see the history of the distortion of our imagery. I'm talking about something that has nothing to do with nostalgia. Within that story there is the total history of my oppression and my refusal to be oppressed."

"I think I may be like you," Anna said. "I too have undergone a radical reorientation toward existence."

Then Anna thought of a short poem about being like Dora.

Modesty itself is a temptation
like dry earth, rough tongue
you, like me.
Honeysuckle. Steam
A blue-gray scalding hiss.

All night they talked about what living is like.

Later, Anna got out that old book *Romantic Sentences* that Mrs. Noren had given her. There she wrote:

– Fingering your sticky little ears.
– Under her skin there are capillaries. The blood moseys along.
– There is milk in there somewhere. Maybe her throat.
– Orange peel.

"I want to write on your face with Magic Marker," Anna said. "It is so in front of me."

Chapter Twenty-eight

One morning Anna woke up to Dora kissing her on the cheek.

"Do you know why you've been so confused?" Dora asked.

"Do you know why you've lived with such dread and undefined anticipation? Why the world changed so fast every day that you didn't know how to help it? Why you had no explanation?"

"Why?" Anna asked.

"Because, darling," she said, "we've been living in a country on the brink of war."

It was January 16, 1991, the day after Martin Luther King's birthday. Never before had Anna experienced the beginning of a war. As far as Vietnam goes, she had been born into it. Never before had a president announced exactly what day the war would begin and then the people waited for that day to come. Anna and Dora woke up *that day* and turned on the radio waiting for the war to start. Anna regretted, for once, not having a TV, but there was something comforting about huddling around the radio just like her parents did in 1942.

It was a little after six and Anna was boiling water. The radio mentioned a flash over Baghdad and that it had begun. Then, at nine o'clock, the president came on and declared his contempt for his own people. At ten-thirty Anna and Dora went out in the slight drizzle, the kind that was much too warm for January. They walked up First Avenue to the United Nations for the first demonstration on the first night of the war.

There were so many fears in Anna's heart. She feared for her own life. She feared for the lives of others. She feared her own complicity and the complicity of others. She feared all their lives changing faster without the knowledge of how they would change. She feared there would be no change.

"I thought I was going to die of AIDS," said the man protesting next to her. "But now it seems I might die more communally."

This is what it was like, that night, to be an American.

Wherever people are at the moment of war, that is where they have placed themselves. It is a big spotlight.

People sat on buses and in audiences with earphones listening to the news, then focused only on the tiniest details. Little forget-me-nots, forget-mes. Some warm water. A nap. A sweet tooth. A little scratch. A moon for a minute. A soup.

"I would give anything to fuck her," is an apocalyptic thought.

Anna and Dora stood together in the light of the United Nations facing two hundred policemen in riot gear, listening to boring speeches and feeling panic. They could not know that the fear and anticipation they felt would be quickly surrounded by an institutionalized narcoleptic nationalism and widespread boredom. They could not know that all Americans would spend the next few weeks glued to twenty-four-hour news reports that told them absolutely nothing. They could not know that within three days the entire nation would be wearing little yellow ribbons on their lapels as though their children were playing football instead of imposing mass death.

Soon, one hundred and seventy-five thousand Iraqi people would be massacred in a computerized war that would be presented to the American people like a video game. The numbers of Iraqi dead would never be mentioned. Their destruction would never be acknowledged. More Americans would be killed by guns in New York City during the war than would be killed in the Gulf. But afterward, soldiers who had used tanks to plow desert sands into trenches where Iraqis were buried alive, these same soldiers, would be hailed on those New York City streets as heroes. All over America, these soldiers would be paraded and rewarded and then forgotten to the unemployment lines, with no health insurance and no future. In fact, the entire war would be forgotten. It would inspire no books, no songs, no metaphors for right and wrong. A year later a famous fashion photographer would do a fabulous spread on the generals for an exclusive glamour magazine. Anyone remembering to ask what the war was like would probably hear a drunken regurgitated slogan like: "If you want freedom, you gotta fight for it, man."

The entire shape of the world's geography would change. The meaning would not be clear and its beneficiaries would remain obscured. Huge numbers of people would lose the rights they had only recently won on paper, and which had never had time to actually be enforced. There would be a shift in the way people lived.

But Dora and Anna could not know this on the night of January 16, 1991. They were living in a prewar period that could not be identified until the war itself was acknowledged. But the real war was ongoing. The real war was at home. The real war had not been televised. All Anna and Dora knew was that this was a moment in history whose outcome could not be imagined. And so they looked through the drizzle into the lights with very simple and simplistic understanding.

"I just figured out the reason for the Cold War," Anna said.

"What?"

"The reason for the Cold War was not to keep the Soviets in check. The reason was to keep us in check."

"I was just thinking something like that myself," Dora said.

Chapter Twenty-nine

FADE IN

INT. RUTH AND IRV'S APARTMENT. LATE EVENING. PASSOVER.

The family is sitting around a seder table set up in the living room. It is obvious from the clutter on the table that they have just finished the meal and are preparing to resume the seder.

RUTH

(*Getting up to clear the table.*)
Anybody want more coffee? I'll make another pot.

ANNA

Ma, let Stevie clear the table. Steve, clear the table.

STEVE

Don't tell me what to do.

ANNA

(*Getting up to clear the table.*)
I just don't see why, in this family in 1991, men still don't clear the table.

BARB

I'll clear the table.

ANNA

What's the matter, Barbara? You don't like conflict?

RUTH

You, you shouldn't lift a single plate. You didn't eat a thing. You didn't even eat the parsley. What's wrong with you?

ANNA

Obviously she's anorexic.

SYLVIA

Remember the way my Zeyde used to dovan all night?

IRV

Yeah. Those were the good old days.

SYLVIA

You and me and Morris would fall asleep under the table.

STEVE

Let's start on the second part of the seder. I have an hour on the subway after all of this.

SYLVIA

Okay, you gotta find the afikomon. Find the matzah and Daddy will give you a big reward.

IRV

Yeah, you can have anything you want under a dollar.
(*Laughs.*)

RUTH

There's no more children in this family. Where are the grandchildren?

SYLVIA

Ruthie, it's a new age.

RUTH

No grandchildren is a new age?

SYLVIA

What do you want? That's progress.

STEVE

I'm gonna be thirty in two weeks. I'm a full professor in Cinema Studies and I have a book on Paul DeMan coming out in the fall. I'm too old to look for the matzah.

ANNA

But you're not too old to clear the table.

IRV

We can't start the seder without the matzah.

SYLVIA

You're all a bunch of stinkers. I'll find it.

SYLVIA *starts looking for the matzah.*

IRV

I remember when my Zeyde used to hide it in his butter churn. A butter churn! Steve, I bet you don't even know what that is.

STEVE

I know more than you think.

BARB

What's a butter churn?

SYLVIA

I got it! Irv, that was too simple. You put it in the most obvious place.

IRV

Where? I forgot where I put it.

BARB

What's a butter churn?

SYLVIA

I forgot too.

RUTH

Okay, Sylvia, what do you want?

BARB

Yeah, Sylvia, come up with something good.

SYLVIA

I want everyone around the table to say their seder wish. I'll start. I wish my daughter will be safe and happy in the Peace Corps.

IRV

Where is she again?

SYLVIA

Gabon.

IRV

Gabon.

SYLVIA

And I hope she comes home soon and that next year she'll be here with us at seder. Now, Barbara, what is your wish?

BARB

I wish for all wars to end. I wish for peace on earth for everyone.

RUTH

I wish the Israelis would give back the land already. But only the West Bank. For years the Arabs threatened to bomb Israel. But only George Bush could actually make them do it. And that the whole family should be healthy and that I should have grandchildren while I'm still healthy enough to enjoy them.

STEVE

I wish that the whole family should be healthy. I think that's a good wish.

SYLVIA

Irv?

IRV

Physical health is very important. But, more important is how you feel about yourself. Like Ruthie says, we all need to be free inside. Even the Palestinians must be free.

BARB

Anna?

ANNA

I wish my friends would stop dying of AIDS.

RUTH

You always have to bring that up.

SYLVIA

Shush, Ruthie, it's her turn.

ANNA

And I wish something I'd rather keep private.

IRV

Okay, that's it. You know, it's very interesting. Seders are not really about telling the story of how we were slaves in Egypt.

BARB

What are they really about, Pop?

IRV

I think that they are more of a way of ensuring that the family psychology is kept dynamic. We all sit down together and take a good look at each other.

SYLVIA

And, God willing, we'll all be here next year to do it again.

RUTH

God has nothing to do with it.

Phone rings.

IRV

I'll get it. It may be a patient.

IRV *exits.*

RUTH

And I hope I never see a yellow ribbon again for as long as I live. Ron Silliman calls them "soft swastikas." That's what they are, soft swastikas.

IRV *comes back.*

BARB

What is it, Pop?

IRV

It's an emergency. I've got to go to the hospital.

BARB

Not again.

STEVE

Well, that about wraps up this seder.

RUTH

Irv, take a cab.

IRV

Of course I'll take a cab.

INT. HALLWAY OF THE BUILDING

IRV *is waiting for the elevator.* ANNA *comes down the hallway, still holding her napkin.*

IRV

What's the matter?

ANNA

Pop, I want to tell you something.

IRV

I've got an emergency.

ANNA

Pop, I just wanted to let you know that I realize you believe in Freud and everything, and I'm not going to go into that right now.

IRV

I don't have that much time right now.

ANNA

I know. But I Just want to tell you that, despite what Freud says, the reason I am a lesbian is not because of wanting to hurt you. It's not about you in any way. I really love you, Pop, and I'm a lot like you and being a lesbian is about me. Okay?

IRV

I'm glad to hear that you love me. Sometimes I'm not too sure.

The elevator arrives.

IRV

Ooops, gotta go. I have an emergency at the hospital. I think I'd better take a cab.

ANNA

Pop, it's after eleven. Don't take the subway, take a cab.

THE END

Chapter Thirty

That night Anna put her head on Dora's breast and something changed. It had to do with the dusty apartment and the expression in the other's face. It was the opposite of talking.

If I doubted you, I'd be glued to the floor by fear.

But instead there was a bending at the neck and Dora's two hands flat up against her lover's chest.

So, Anna decided not to be an asshole anymore, which meant having to ruin her own reputation. But the verbal police were talking and she couldn't say, "No, officer, what contraband?" Because … because … because she had a chance for happiness and so put out her hand to reach for the real right thing.

Why?

For the sake of affection and mutual knowledge. For the sake of a fearful future and the little "ooh" that pops in her chest when Anna sees this woman's real face and not that strange memory of some empress, flushed. And two breasts in the process of being made love to, pulled freely out of a torn striped shirt. These torn stripes light up the whole picture and give some geometry to an otherwise experiential image.

When I put my hand inside her there is a waiting room filled with amiable travelers. When she comes, they go and pass us by. One is a lanky guy – stringy hair to the shoulders. One is a quiet shuffler – always looks at his feet.

Eyes that were full of trains. Hair that was full of trains. Air travel is meaningless, merits no comparisons but these women had trains for veins. Clacking late nights, passing bright lights, and cigarettes out the windows of strangers' compartments. Anna came out of the movie and found it had rained. The sidewalk was wet.

Appendices

What I've learned about *Empathy*
by Sarah Schulman

The MacDowell Colony, August 15, 2005

I'm trying to remember when I first got interested in juxtaposition, which is the experience at the core of this novel: relations between ideas, word fragments, genres, lovers, and relational existence as a fallback position for people whose reality is not acknowledged. Homosexually, it probably began in my 1962 nursery school class. Our young teacher was getting married, and she organized us into a mass mock wedding. The four-year-olds had to couple up boy/girl, boy/girl and march down the aisle. I refused. I said I would be the photographer, and ran around with an invisible camera, snapping non-existent pictures. I existed, in that moment as a lesbian and an artist, relationally. There was no girlfriend and no apparatus, yet I survived as myself, a not-bride.

Artistically, Jean Genet and Joni Mitchell, who I adored all through high school, modeled the strength of unusual word relationships creating a third space of depth. In college it was Sun Ra, and the Art Ensemble of Chicago. They helped me grasp and romance the work of Patti Smith when I returned to New York. There was Robert Altman's *Nashville* which I've seen fifteen times. It taught me the excitement of a story you can't understand until you've finished it. Then, suddenly, you need to go back and read/see it again. In the early 1980s, I was a waitress at Leroy's Restaurant, the only coffee shop in the still-industrial Tribeca. Meredith Monk lived across the street and she used to come in for breakfast. Meredith decided to do her new piece, *Turtle Dreams* (still available on CD) cabaret style, so she hired a bunch of us to serve drinks to the audience. I had never seen a work of art like this one before. I recall it as a hopeful, optimistic collection of syllables (my favorite song had the refrain "Wella Kalay, Wella Kalay") accompanied by precise arm and leg movements similar to Charlie Chaplin's factory gestures in *Modern Times* delivered with panache. Although this was a new language for me, after waitressing many performances, the ordered sounds crept into my heart. When my first novel, *The Sophie Horowitz Story*, was published by Naiad Press in 1984, an interviewer asked about my use of "pastiche." I didn't know what that word meant. I guess I had already learned postmodernism organically.

Sex also brought me fragments. A relationship with choreographer Susan Seizer (who I met in bed with a third party in 1979), introduced me to postmodern dance. I also had a simultaneous relationship with filmmaker Abigail Child, who introduced me to experimental film in an intense and intimate way. The lesbian culture of this era was very rich sexually, and as I re-read *Empathy*, I see evidence of many different kinds of sexual experiences I had with a wide range of women. The three-way in the opening pages is absolutely accurate. An alcoholic cowgirl (who I had sex with) said the words, "the subway makes speeches under our feet." My girlfriend while I was writing this book (who I met on the subway), Debby Karpel, a singer, was the lovely office temp whose co-worker complained to her about a gay man sitting too close to him. "How would you like it if some butchy woman was in your face all night long?" Anna O.'s femininity was partially hers.

I was working, on a daily basis, interdisciplinarily with composers, dancers, filmmakers, choreographers, designers, performance artists. From 1979 to 1994, I was involved in fifteen collaborative shows as part of the Downtown Arts Movement located in the East Village. In 1986, Jim Hubbard and I founded the New York Lesbian and Gay Experimental Film Festival (now called *Mix*), so I spent many years watching gay artists express their realities far from the world of realism. There I found a deeper, truer story than anything available on television or in the movies. As the AIDS crisis crashed into our world, fragments became more and more the only authentic conveyor of lived experience.

Yet, in the late eighties, when I started to write *People in Trouble* (Dutton, 1990), I chose classic realism. I remember this process very clearly. I was embarking on what I thought would be a new kind of American literature: witness fiction. The AIDS crisis had been in full force since 1981, and had produced shocked, desperate, half-baked books by grasping, dying people, or shattered lovers of the dying anticipating their own inevitable demise. I was none of the above, and yet lived in the eye of the hurricane, and I wanted to write a book that would explain the disease in dynamic relationship to the political movement it spawned. Strangely, the subsequent AIDS works that have become iconic in our culture rarely mention the movement, or the engaged community of lovers, but both formations were inseparable from the crisis itself. Now, looking back, I fear that the story of the isolated helpless homosexual was one far more palatable to the corporations who control the reward system in the arts. The more truthful story of the American mass – abandoning families, criminal governments, indifferent neighbors – is too uncomfortable and inconvenient to recall. The story of how gay people who were despised, had no rights, and carried the burden of a terrible disease came together to force the country to change against its will, is apparently too implicating to tell. Fake tales of individual heterosexuals heroically overcoming their prejudices to rescue helpless dying men with AIDS was a lot more appealing to the powers that be, but not at all true.

I had a complex moment to convey. I remember re-reading Zola's *Germinal*, and realizing that my story, too, needed a flat surface texture to be understood. So I wrote clear, distinct sentences. Crafted a conventional narrative structure. I cleanly divided the novel into three characters' individual points of view, neatly indicated by whichever name appeared at the top of each chapter. It was an exercise in restraint towards a larger goal. That novel did its job (for a lot more juicy information about the fate of *People in Trouble* see *Stagestruck: Theater, AIDS, and the Marketing of Gay America*, Duke University Press, 1998), but I was very unsatisfied artistically. The book was effective in its moment, and I know that I made the only choice I could make. But by the time *Empathy* came around, I was exploding with impulse towards the mysteries that experimentation can express, which are often lost in the conventions of naturalism.

Now for the materialist side of this story.

I probably started writing *Empathy* in 1989, a good time for me professionally. I had had a great victory with my 1988 novel *After Delores* (Dutton), the first modern lesbian novel to be published by a mainstream press and gloriously received on its own terms in the *New York Times*. *People in Trouble* was also treated with respect and decency, and artistically I was feeling quite confident. So confident, in fact, that when my editor for both novels, Carole DeSanti, was temporarily fired from my publisher, Dutton, I was able to get in my contract for *Empathy* that she was to be hired on a freelance basis to edit the book.

The earliest piece of *Empathy* was a term paper I wrote for Professor Bert Cohler at the University of Chicago in 1976, where I used Freud's *Interpretation of Dreams* to show that I was a lesbian. He gave me an A-. It was a brave thing to do on my part, and an extraordinary act of kindness on his. Homosexuality, especially one's own, was considered inappropriate classroom subject matter at that time and place. I had no openly gay teachers, only a handful of openly gay students on the entire campus, and a great books curriculum that included only one woman, Sappho. This was why many people of my generation who wanted to be out in their work left the academy. Many of those who stayed often had to do closeted dissertations or first books in order to get jobs and/or tenure, and then were able to come out in their scholarly endeavors. Ironically, that same semester, I took a course called "Images of Women in French Literature," in which the female professor said that "whether a writer is a lesbian or not is as important as if she's right-handed or left-handed." I also had a course on "Freud and Literary Criticism" in which the professor said, "We all know that female students contribute nothing to a classroom situation," and forbade us to write papers on feminism. Cohler's decency was so unusual, and so enormously helpful in allowing me to become myself. I dropped out of that school and went to Hunter College to study with Audre Lorde. But thirty years later, I returned to the Chicago campus and actually saw Professor Cohler, now elderly and emeritus. I was able to tell him how much he had helped me, and thank him. He told me that he himself was now openly gay, and that his gay students now have much more freedom to discuss their truths in the classroom. He was concerned about their difficulties with relationships, and how much pain that causes them. I was moved again by his compassionate heart.

I suppose the original study for *Empathy* was my one and only published short story, "The Penis Story" (which is anthologized in *Chloe Plus Olivia*, edited by Lillian Faderman), in which a sexually seductive but withholding straight woman does so much psychic damage to a lesbian that she wakes up one morning with a penis. This puts her in high demand sexually with other women, but the way they make love is called "glancing." The story was written in 1979, but rejected by literary magazines for years. In fact, I received rejection letters signed by Adrienne Rich for *Sinister Wisdom*, and Dorothy Allison for *Conditions*. It was eventually published by Susie Bright in *on our backs*, which was an odd trajectory for me because I've never been this super-sexy or sexually performative person; that is not my way of being outrageous. This story just came a bit too early for the zeitgeist, three years before the infamous Barnard College Scholar and the Feminist Conference where the internal pornography debates exploded and fractured the community into warring factions for decades. I was very much on the outside of those battles, not identifying with either position. I've always been turned off by the various "sex radical" factions that have waxed and waned over the years. They often seemed rather grim, and weirdly repressed. We all have sex, after all.

I started writing this novel from a very deep place of authority within myself. I did not know what the book was about, I did not "know" what I was grappling with. I just really believed in myself and with this, my fifth novel, felt very comfortable writing. In fact, I was the freest I have ever been as a writer, in that I was able to write without needing to predetermine the script. The discovery was, literally, in the writing. To help the book I read transformative literature: two *Metamorphoses* are cited, those of Ovid and Kafka, who wrote "Gregor Samsa awoke from unsettling dreams," and who gave me the existence of Herr K. I looked at Georgia O'Keefe ("A red mask. A red egg. A moonscape made of glass." – which I used again in *Rat Bohemia*). Other influences I can see as I re-read: James Schuyler ("boxy trucks") and Wilhelm Reich ("the basic function of all living creatures is to expand and contract").

I did twelve drafts of *Empathy*. The book contains, I believe, eight different forms: screenplay, short story, play, recipe, personal ad, advertisements, term paper, poem (my first of only two). I did not realize that the collection of multiple forms was, itself, part of the statement of the novel about the state of lesbian existence. And I can honestly say that I did not know that the book was about the desire to exist until the tenth draft. I wrote for at least two years, just trusting myself. And then the revelation was unveiled. The "secret," or narrative twist revealed near the end of the novel, was something I myself only learned on draft ten. Then I suddenly realized that I had been writing in a deeply truthful way, directly from my unconscious, facing issues that I was personally not ready to grapple with consciously. Only by giving myself enormous permission to not have clarity in the piece for so long, was the ultimate clarity able to be achieved.

I was very excited by the book. I felt that there was a new maturity of voice that could only have been realized as a consequence of having written so much already. At that point, with five novels, several plays, and many journalistic works, I probably had invented more lesbian characters than any writer in the history of the world, and had more experience with lesbian representation than any of my predecessors. I had a deep knowledge of the mechanics of that representation and I felt it was flourishing into an exciting new sophistication both literary and social. Pre-publication was interesting as well. The original title, *Empathy, The Cheapest of Emotions* had to be changed because the marketing department at Dutton felt that it sounded like a self-help book. The cover was my first computer-generated graphic, and I loved that. The blurbs started to come in, interesting comments from interesting people. Kate Millet called this stylization an "American thought sentence," which I loved, not only because she correctly identified that third place between speech and feeling, but because she called my writing "American," taking it out of the second-class position of being considered special interest. Fay Weldon sent in her blurb, "The lesbian novel comes of age." I hoped that this revelation, of gender position as a state of mind, would begin a whole new discourse, an exciting conversation in which we would have some control of the ways we understood ourselves. I wanted formal authority. My dear friend Rachel Pollack, a novelist, tarot card master, and transsexual heroine, loved the book. And her praise meant so much to me. She particularly responded to the words "a lesbian trapped in a woman's body" as both a statement of truth and a refutation of the reductionist phrase "woman trapped in a man's body" that transsexuals had had to endure. But she also knew that it was a response, as well, to the provocative statement of genius Monique Wittig: "I am not a woman, I'm a lesbian." The future seemed full of promise.

But.

The success of *After Delores* allowed my editor Carole to publish more lesbian novels, and she developed a significant list of good writers willing to engage lesbian content with integrity. Lesbian subjectivity was increasingly present in the mainstream book business, primarily due to Dutton, and occasional titles from St. Martin's and a few other houses publishing such exciting novels as Carol Anshaw's *Aquamarine*, Carolivia Herron's *Thereafter Johnny*, plus British imports dominated by the work of Jeanette Winterson. But an unspoken, and I now believe unrecognized, discomfort with the normalization of lesbian life started to become expressed through marketing techniques that firmly, though surreptitiously, re-relegated these works to second-class status. The chain booksellers, like Barnes and Noble, began to dominate the market, and they instituted a "gay and lesbian" section in many of their branch stores. This section was never positioned at the front of the store with the bestsellers. It was usually on the fourth floor hidden behind the potted plants. What this meant in practical terms was that those of us who had the integrity to be out in our work found our books literarily yanked off of the "Fiction" shelves and hidden on the gay shelves, where only "gay" people wanting "gay" books would dare to tread. It was an instant undoing of all the progress we had made to be treated as full citizens and a natural, organic part of American intellectual life.

While community-based gay, lesbian, and feminist bookstores had always been the backbone of our literature, devoted to books published by independent presses, I had – at this point – been a mainstream author for years. I felt very strongly, and still do, that authentic lesbian literature should be represented at all levels of publishing, including taking its rightful place as a natural organic part of mainstream American intellectual life. The corporate lockdown went into overdrive just at the moment that this integration was beginning to take place. This positioning is essential for so many reasons, least of which is the right of writers of merit to not be excluded from financial, emotional, and intellectual development simply because they have the integrity to be out in their work. Second is the right of gay people to be in dialogic relationships with straights – where they read and identify with our work as we are asked to with theirs. And finally, that even at the height of the strength of the lesbian subculture, most gay people find out about gay things through the mainstream media.

In this crucial year, 1992, Dutton, and perhaps other publishers of gay male literature, hired gay people to market their gay books to other gay people. In other words, they created a two-tiered marketing system. When *After Delores* had been published, there was no gay substructure inside mainstream publishing, so the book was treated like a book. It was reviewed by a heterosexual man, Kinky Friedman, for the *Times*. At the time, Dutton didn't even collect review clippings from gay newspapers. Now, with an iron-handed containment system starting to be put into place, gay books were increasingly reviewed by gay people. And reviewing publications clearly had unarticulated but lethal quota systems for how many lesbian books they would review. So that authors were competing against each other for review space, simply on the basis of being out in their work even when the books had absolutely nothing else in common. Gay authors were, in turn, often asked to review gay books with which they were not aesthetically compatible. The fact of being out in one's work became the single most determining factor in how a woman's career would be allowed to develop. *Empathy* was published in 1992. That same year, Dutton published a novel by an openly lesbian author, but the novel had no primary lesbian content. It was called *Bastard Out of Carolina*. And the two books were put on different marketing tiers. I was put on the newly created gay marketing track, sold only to other gay people. *Bastard* was treated like a regular book, one that straight people would be offered. An experienced book promoter, with four US tours and British, German, Dutch, and Japanese book tours under my belt, I was rather shocked to see the press list I received from the well-meaning gay Dutton publicist newly hired to sell gay books to gay people only. Almost all of the interviews were with gay venues. I had one straight radio interview, and the fellow asked me what it was like to be "a lesbian who doesn't hate men." When I called Carole, we discovered that that phrase had appeared on the Dutton press release. It was the advent of niche marketing, which basically guaranteed that the brief window of being treated like a human, when in fact I was actually just a lesbian, had come to an end.

I have to say honestly that in that moment, I did not exactly understand what was going on. I also had my own agenda which was not immediately thwarted by the permanent shift towards containment marketing. 1992 was also the year that myself and five other women founded the direct action movement, The Lesbian Avengers, an anarchist explosion that went from a few New Yorkers imagining parachuting into Whitney Houston's wedding, to twenty-two chapters on four continents within two years, and then crashed and burned. (See *My American History: Lesbian and Gay Life During the Reagan/Bush Years*, Routledge, 1994 for more information.) At that time, I was a particular kind of person. I believed in the Marxist dictum, "Each according to their ability, each according to their need." Often, I was the one with the ability, and so I gave hugely and consistently, believing that if the day should come when I was the one with the need, it would be reciprocated. I did not yet understand the consequence of oppression on people's emotional lives. And I also did not deeply accept that in many ways I am an exceptional person, able and willing to do things that others won't do. This has been a very difficult lesson for me to learn. I am willing to be uncomfortable for a higher purpose, and that is not a capacity shared by many other people, which is a source of great pain to me. After all, it was the willingness to write in the discomfort of unknowing for two years that allowed this novel to come to be. But in 1992, this had not all been revealed, and so I decided *according to my ability* to use my *Empathy* book tour to recruit Lesbian Avenger chapters around the country. I requested a tour of all the gay bookstores in the US South. Actually, I requested the tour budget, and constructed the tour myself. I read from *Empathy* and tried to start Lesbian Avenger chapters in Atlanta, New Orleans, Birmingham, Huntsville, Greensboro, Raleigh/Durham, Austin, and a number of other locations through to Los Angeles and up to San Francisco. Some of these chapters took hold, others came to be through second starts some months later, and others didn't take at all. But in the end, it was a very successful tour for the Avenger movement.

While the Avengers resonated with people's needs and interests, the doors that I thought that *Empathy* would open about gender turned out to be entirely out of step with the historic moment. Instead, the zeitgeist was pointing in other directions. Judith Butler, someone who I like and respect, published *Gender Trouble*, which argued persuasively for gender as something presentational. My book tour of Germany coincided with hers, and every place I arrived, she had just departed. People kept asking in German accents, "But isn't gender performative?" I found her followers to be sort of annoying. Kate Bornstein and Leslie Feinberg also published significant books which extended the discussion of gender in the direction of body modification, dress, pronouns, and science, i.e. exteriority. The transsexual/transgender revolution was happening in a big way. Usually, when I would go on a book tour, I would ask audiences what lesbian books they loved. The previous year it had been Diane DiMassa's *Hothead Paisan*. Suddenly, every other dyke was reading *Stone Butch Blues.* The tide had turned in exactly the opposite direction from my own private revelations about the lesbian self. And the shift seemed permanent. Some years later, I heard Judith Halberstam speak at the Whitney Museum on her theory of "Female Masculinity." I was very confused by her thesis, and raised my hand to ask, "Why do you say that butch is masculine?" I'd always experienced it as a highly feminine state. Everyone seemed to understand but me. The group conscience was going the other way. As Sun Ra said, "You're on the right road but you're going in the wrong direction." In the subsequent decade, more women have decided to transition and become men through body modification. As *Empathy* expresses, I have never personally experienced any similarity between lesbians and men. To me, lesbians and men were on opposite ends of "the continuum."

Even years later when I fell in love and experienced mutual sexual ecstasy and joy with a woman who had a transgendered identity, her maleness did not express itself in public presentation or body-modification. It was only in her soul. I gave her *Empathy*, but she never read it. Neither, apparently, did many other people. *Empathy* was my worst-selling book, the least reviewed (the *Times* ignored it), and the least translated (three foreign editions: Sheba, UK; Argument Verlag, Germany; Alfaguara, Spain). It has provoked the fewest Masters theses, doctoral dissertations, and chapters in academic books of any of my work. It is rarely taught. In short, it flopped.

But I love it. *Empathy* is my free, wild child, the book I wrote from my deepest most optimistic place with my greatest skill. And I am so grateful to Arsenal Pulp Press for rescuing it from the recycling bin. Maybe this time around, it will make more sense to someone other than me.

From *Chloe Plus Olivia: An Anthology of Lesbian Literature from the Seventeenth Century to the Present*, edited by Lillian Faderman (Viking Penguin, 1994)

"The Penis Story" by Sarah Schulman, 1979

The night before they sat in their usual spots. Jesse's hair was like torrents of black oil plunging into the sea. Ann watched her, remembering standing in the butcher shop looking at smoked meat, smelling the grease, imagining Jesse's tongue on her labia. She was starving.

"I'm just waiting for a man to rescue me," Jesse said.

"Look, Jess," Ann answered. "Why don't we put a timeline on this thing. Let's say forty. If no man rescues you by the time you're forty, we'll take it from a different angle. What do you say?"

"I say I'll be in a mental hospital by the time I'm forty."

Jesse was thirty-two. This was a realistic possibility.

"Jesse, if instead of being two women, you and I were a woman and a man, would we be lovers by now?"

"Yes." Jess had to answer yes because it was so obviously true.

"So what's not there for you in us being two women? Is it something concrete about a man, or is it the idea of a man?"

"I don't think it's anything physical. I think it is the idea of a man. I want to know that my lover is a man. I need to be able to say that."

Ann started to shake and covered her legs with a blanket so it wouldn't be so obvious. She felt like a child. She put her head on Jesse's shoulder feeling weak and ridiculous. Then they kissed. It felt so familiar. They'd been doing that for months. Each knew how the other kissed. Ann felt Jesse's hand on her waist and back and chest. Jesse reached her hand to Ann's bra. She'd done this before too. First tentatively, then more directly, she brushed her hands and face against Ann's breasts. Ann kissed her skin and licked it. She sucked her fingers, knowing those nails would have to be cut if Jesse were to ever put her fingers into Ann's body. She looked at Jesse's skin, at her acne scars and blackheads. She wanted to kiss her a hundred times. Then, as always, Jesse became disturbed, agitated. "I'm nervous again," she said. "Like, *oh no – now I'm going to have to fuck*."

Suddenly Ann remembered that their sexual life together was a piece of glass. She put on her shirt and went home. This was the middle of the night in New York City.

When Ann awoke the next morning from unsettling dreams, she saw that a new attitude had dawned with the new day. She felt accepting, not proud. She felt ready to face adjustment and compromise. She was ready for change. Even though she was fully awake her eyes had not adjusted to the morning. She reached for glasses but found them inadequate. Then she looked down and saw that she had a penis.

Surprisingly, she didn't panic. Ann's mind, even under normal circumstances, worked differently than the minds of many of those around her. She was able to think three thoughts at the same time, and as a result often suffered from headaches, disconnected conversation, and too many ideas. However, at this moment she only had two thoughts: "What is it going to be like to have a penis?" and "I will never be the same again."

It didn't behave the way most penises do. It rather seemed to be trying to find its own way. It swayed a bit as she walked to the bathroom mirror, careful not to let her legs interfere, feeling off balance, as if she had an itch and couldn't scratch it. She tried to sit back on her hips, for she still had hips, and walk pelvis first, for she still had her pelvis. In fact, everything appeared to be the same except that she had no vagina. Except that she had a prick.

"I am a prick," she said to herself.

The first thing she needed to do was piss and that was fun, standing up seeing it hit the water, but it got all over the toilet seat and she had to clean up the yellow drops.

"I am a woman with a penis and I am still cleaning up piss."

This gave her a sense of historical consistency. Now it was time to get dressed.

She knew immediately that she didn't want to hide her penis from the world. Ann had never hidden anything else, no matter how controversial. There was nothing wrong with having a penis. Men had them and now she did too. She wasn't going to let her penis keep her from the rest of humanity. She chose a pair of button-up Levi's and stuffed her penis into her pants where it bulged pretty obviously. Then she put on a t-shirt that showed off her breasts and her muscles and headed toward the F train to Shelley's house to meet her friends for lunch.

By the time Ann finished riding on the F train she had developed a fairly integrated view of her new self. She was a lesbian with a penis. She was not a man with breasts. She was a woman. This was not androgyny, she'd never liked that word. Women had always been whole to Ann, not half of something waiting to be completed.

They sat in Shelley's living room eating lunch. These were her most attentive friends, the ones who knew best how she lived. They sat around joking until Shelley finally asked, "What's that between your legs?"

"That's my penis," Ann said.

"Oh, so now you have a penis."

"I got it this morning. I woke up and it was there."

They didn't think much of Ann's humor usually, so the conversation moved on to other topics. Judith lit a joint. They got high and said funny things, but they did keep coming back to Ann's penis.

"What are you going to do with it?" Shelley asked.

"I don't know."

"If you really have a penis, why don't you show it to us?" Roberta said. She was always provocative.

Ann remained sitting in her chair but unbuttoned her jeans and pulled her penis out of her panties. She had balls too.

"Is that real?"

Roberta came over and put her face in Ann's crotch. She held Ann's penis in her hands. It just lay there.

"Yup, Ann's got a penis all right."

"Did you eat anything strange yesterday?" Judith asked.

"Maybe it's from masturbating," Roberta suggested, but they all knew that couldn't be true.

"Well, Ann, let me know if you need anything, but I have to say I'm glad we're not lovers anymore because I don't think I could handle this." Judith bit her lip.

"I'm sure you'd do fine," Ann replied in her usual charming way.

Ann put on her flaming electronic lipstick. It smudged accidentally, but she liked the effect. This was preparation for the big event. Ann was ready to have sex. Thanks to her lifelong habit of masturbating before she went to sleep, Ann had sufficiently experimented with erections and come. She'd seen enough men do it and knew how to do it for them, so she had no trouble doing it for herself. Sooner or later she would connect with another person. Now was that time. She wore her t-shirt that said, "Just visiting from another planet." Judith had given it to her and giggled, nervously.

The Central Park Ramble used to be a bird and wildlife sanctuary. Because it's hidden, and therefore foreboding, gay men use it to have sex, and that's where Ann wanted to be. Before she had a penis, Ann used to imagine sometimes while making love that she and her girlfriend were two gay men. Now that she had this penis, she felt open to different kinds of people and new ideas, too.

She saw a gay man walking through the park in his little gym suit. He had a nice tan like Ann did and a gold earring like she did too. His t-shirt also had writing on it. It said, "All-American Boy." His ass stuck out like a mating call.

"Hi," she said.

"Hi," he said.

"Do you want to smoke a joint?" she asked very sweetly.

He looked around suspiciously.

"Don't worry, I'm gay too."

"OK honey, why not. There's nothing much happening anyway."

So, they sat down and smoked a couple of joints and laughed and told about the different boyfriends and girlfriends that they had had, and which ones had gone straight and which ones had broken their hearts. Then Ann produced two beers and they drank those and told about the hearts that they had broken. It was hot and pretty in the park.

Ann mustered up all her courage and said.

"I have a cock."

"You look pretty good for a mid-op," he said.

His name was Mike.

"No, I'm not transsexual, I'm a lesbian with a penis. I know this is unusual, but would you suck my cock?"

Ann had always wanted to say "suck my cock" because it was one thing a lot of people said to her and she never said to anyone. Once she and her friends made little stickers that said "End Violence in the Lives of Women," which they stuck up all over the subway. Many mornings when she was riding to work, Ann would see that different people had written over them "suck my cock." It seemed like an appropriate response given the world in which we all live.

Mike thought this was out of the ordinary, but he prided himself on taking risks. So he decided "what the hell" and went down on her like an expert.

Well, it did feel nice. It didn't feel like floating in hot water, which is what Ann sometimes thought of when a woman made love to her well with her mouth, but it did feel good. She started thinking about other things. She tried to two-gay-men image but it had lost its magic. Then she remembered Jesse. She saw them together in Jesse's apartment. Each in their usual spots.

"What's the matter, Annie? Your face is giving you away."

"This is such a bastardized version of how I'd like to be relating to you right now."

"Well," said Jesse. "What would it be like?"

"Oh, I'd be sitting here and you'd say 'I'm ready' and I'd say, 'ready for what?' and you'd say, 'I'm ready to make love to you, Annie.' Then I'd say 'Why don't we go to your bed?' and we would."

"Yes," Jesse said. "I would smell your smell, Annie. I would put my arms on your neck and down over your breasts. I would unbutton your shirt, Annie, and pull it off your shoulders. I would run my fingers down your neck and over your nipples. I would lick your breasts, Annie, I would run my tongue down your neck to your breasts.'

Ann could feel Jess's wild hair like the ocean passing over her chest. Jesse's mouth was on her nipples licking, her soft face against Ann's skin. She was licking, licking then sucking harder and faster until Jesse clung to her breasts harder and harder.

"You taste just like my wife," Mike said after she came.

"What?"

Ann's heart was beating. The ocean was crashing in her ears.

"I said, you taste just like my wife, when you come I mean. You don't come sperm, you know, you come women's cum, like pussy."

"Oh thank God."

Ann was relieved.

Another morning Ann woke up and her fingers were all sticky. It was still dark. First she thought she'd had a wet dream, but when she turned on her reading lamp she saw blood all over her hands. Instinctively she put her fingers in her mouth. It was gooey, full of membrane and salty. It was her period. She guessed it had no other place to come out, so it flowed from under her fingernails. She spent the next three and a half days wearing black plastic gloves.

The feeling of her uterine lining coming out of her hands gave Ann some hope. After living with her penis for nearly a month, she was beginning to experience it as a loss, not an acquisition. She was grieving for her former self.

One interesting item was that Ann was suddenly in enormous sexual demand. More women than had ever wanted to make love with her wanted her now. But most of them didn't want anyone to know, so she said no.

There was one woman, though, to whom she said yes. Her name was Muriel. Muriel dreamed that she made love to a woman with a penis and it was called "glancing." So she looked high and low until she found Ann, who she believed had a rare and powerful gift and should be honored.

Ann and Muriel became lovers and Ann learned many new things from this experience. She realized that when you meet a woman, you see the parts of her body that she's going to use to make love to you. You see her mouth and teeth and tongue and fingers. You see her fingers comb her hair, play the piano, wash the dishes, write a letter. You watch her mouth eat and whistle and quiver and scream and kiss. When she makes love to you she brings all of this movement and activity with her into your body.

Ann liked this. With her penis, however, it wasn't the same. She had to keep it private. She also didn't like fucking Muriel very much. She missed the old way. Putting her penis into a woman's body was so confusing. Ann knew it wasn't making love "to" Muriel and it certainly wasn't Muriel making love "to" her. It was more like making love "from" Muriel and that just didn't sit right.

One day Ann told Muriel about Jesse.

"I give her everything within my capacity to give and she gives me everything within her capacity to give – only my capacity is larger than hers."

In response Muriel took her to the Museum of Modern Art and pointed to a sculpture by Louise Bourgeois. Ann spent most of the afternoon in front of the large piece, an angry ocean of black penises which rose and crashed, carrying a little box house. The piece was called "Womanhouse." She looked at the penises, their little round heads, their black metal trunks, how they moved together to make waves, and she understood something completely new.

They got together the next day in a bar. As soon as she walked in Ann felt nauseous. She couldn't eat a thing. The smell of grease from Jesse's chicken dinner came in waves to Ann's side of the table. She kept her nose in the beer to cut the stench.

"You're dividing me against myself, Jesse."

Jesse offered her some chicken.

"No thanks, I really don't want any. Look, I can't keep making out with you on a couch because that's as far as you're willing to go before this turns into a lesbian relationship. It makes me feel like nothing."

Ann didn't mention that she had a penis.

"Annie, I can't say I don't love being physical with you because it wouldn't be true."

"I know."

"I feel something ferocious when I smell you. I love kissing you. That's why it's got to stop. I didn't realize when I started this that I was going to want it so much."

"Why is that a problem?"

"Why is that a problem? Why is that a problem?"

Jesse was licking the skin off the bone with her fingers. Slivers of meat stuck out of her long fingernails. She didn't know the answer.

"Jesse, what would happen if someone offered you a woman with a penis?"

Jesse wasn't surprised by this question, because Ann often raised issues from new and interesting perspectives.

"It wouldn't surprise me."

"Why not?"

"Well, Annie, I've never told you this before, actually it's just a secret between me and my therapist, but I feel as though I do have a penis. It's a theoretical penis, in my head. I've got a penis in my head and it's all mine."

"You're right," Ann said. "You do have a penis in your head because you have been totally mind-fucked. You've got an eight-inch cock between your ears."

With that she left the restaurant and left Jesse with the bill.

Soon Ann decided she wanted her clitoris back and she started to consult with doctors who did transsexual surgery. Since Ann had seen, tasted, and touched many clitorises in her short but full life, she knew that each one had its own unique way and wanted her very own cunt back just the way it had always been. So, she called together every woman who had ever made love to her. There was her French professor from college, her brother's girlfriend, her cousin Clarisse, her best friend from high school, Judith, Claudette, Kate, and Jane and assorted others. They all came to a big party at Shelley's house where they got high and drank beer and ate lasagna and when they all felt fine, Ann put a giant piece of white paper on the wall. By committee, they reconstructed Ann's cunt from memory. Some people had been more attentive than others, but they were all willing to make the effort. After a few hours and a couple of arguments as to the exact color tone and how many wrinkles on the left side, they finished the blueprints. "Pussy prints," the figure skater from Iowa City called them.

The following Monday Ann went in for surgery reflecting on the time she had spent with her penis. When you're different, you really have to think about things. You have a lot of information about how the mainstream lives, but they don't know much about you. They also don't know that they don't know, which they don't. Ann wanted one thing, to be a whole woman again. She never wanted to be mutilated by being cut off from herself and she knew that would be a hard thing to overcome, but Ann was willing to try.

From the *Los Angeles Times*, March 7, 1993
"The Anomie Within: *Empathy* by Sarah Schulman"
by John Weir

If personality is just an adjustment to stress, we may all be the result of the crises we survive. The characters in novelist Sarah Schulman's fiction struggle to come to terms with their identity in a contemporary urban landscape that has grown increasingly apocalyptic and implausible. They grasp at love as they watch their friends and lovers die. They strain to understand their lives in the context of global changes and local upheavals. In four previous novels and her current, *Empathy*, Schulman has articulated an ongoing dialogue in which her fictional stand-ins, most often young gay women obsessed with cultural and political concerns, yearn to speak the language of their time, and to learn what actions will suffice in a chaotic world.

"I mean something different in the World than I mean in my world," says Anna O., whose fractured identity is scattered in shards throughout the poignant self-analysis that comprises *Empathy*. She seems to exist only in relationship to her surroundings, or other people. Living in a New York City neighborhood left in disarray by the combination of partial gentrification and increasing poverty that overtook it during the Reagan-Bush years, she is acutely aware of herself as a child of middle-class Jews, "the kind that could pass up just as easily as down." Her word-processing job and visits to her parents help her maintain an illusion of tradition and stability.

She is, after all, an American in whom certain advantages are supposed to inhere automatically. But she is also a gay offspring of vaguely gay-baiting parents, and a woman conditioned from childhood to conceive of her beauty, her sensuality, and her intelligence wholly in comparison to men. Furthermore, she is a child of the '60s, raised to believe in a future that has long since passed into history.

Wondering "what happened to the world I was promised back in the first grade in 1965," she describes what she grew up to expect: "successful middle-class romance, the Jetsons, robots and the metric system." That her life now consists of AIDS, reluctant lovers, crack babies and the homeless is the irony she strives to resolve.

Being able to listen to others and identify with their concerns is Schulman's understanding of empathy, an emotional receptivity that provides Anna with the key to the eventual reintegration of her initially fragmented personality.

If Schulman's structure is complex and sometimes abstruse, her style is refreshingly colloquial. "Simple words are best," the narrator notes, and while Schulman is occasionally guilty of oversimplification, she is most often the master of a gorgeous simplicity that is resilient enough to encompass everything from recipes for Three Musketeers Treasure Puffs to lyrical passages and intimate bedroom chatter. Her gift is her characters' capacity for grace under pressure, and her special charm is her generous, sensual and quite exhilarating observations of women. "Her orgasm was square," Schulman notes, when Anna O. awakes from a sexual dream. "A pink star, a spider web, a dancing star too and a point and a shadow."

Schulman's voice is comic, engaging, alternately hectoring and caressing. It is a New York voice, struggling to liberate itself from received notions about love and identity picked up from Sigmund Freud and Saturday morning cartoons. At times it reminded me of one of Schulman's literary precursors, Delmore Schwartz, a lifelong tortured and effusive New Yorker, a Jewish secular humanist with a broad streak of tenderness beneath his cynicism. "Existentialism means that no one can take a bath for you," Schwartz famously opined. The cosmic loneliness he suffered, comically expressed, reverberates throughout Schulman's writing. But while Schwartz withdrew from the world, retreating into madness, Schulman affirms her connectedness to life, stepping gracefully and conscientiously through the great disorder whirling forever around her.

Excerpts from 'A Person Positions Herself on Quicksand': The Postmodern Politics of Identity and Location in Sarah Schulman's *Empathy*

by Sonya Andermahr, from *'Romancing the Margins'? Lesbian Writing in the 1990s*, edited by Gabriele Griffin (Harrington Park Press, 2000)

Since the advent of the second wave of feminism in the late 1960s, fiction produced by feminist and lesbian writers has provided a powerful engagement with the politics of gender and sexuality. During this period, however, feminist fiction has registered transformations that have affected the theory and practice of feminism more widely. A major shift, dating from the late 1980s, names the theorization of location and the radical rethinking of theories of identity and difference as one of its main concerns. It suggests a reconceptualization of identity, particularly gender identity, from a relatively homogeneous model to a more unstable and heterogeneous conception of what identity means. This requires that feminists take the notion of intrasexual difference – that is difference among women – seriously. All three – theory, politics, fiction – endeavor to offer women ways of simultaneously articulating their differences and challenging inequality. Importantly, they attempt to register both the diversity of women's experiences and the multiplicity of identities within each woman. As a result, the subject fragments, frequently (and sometimes painfully) traversing borders and boundaries, moving across and within culture, history, 'race' and, sometimes, even gender. In this article I want to examine one example of contemporary lesbian feminist fiction – *Empathy* by the US lesbian writer Sarah Schulman – in light of contemporary feminist debates about the politics of location.

In common with much recent feminist fiction by American and British writers such as Jeanette Winterson, Alice Walker, Michele Roberts, and Angela Carter, *Empathy* employs a number of techniques and devices associated with postmodernist and anti-realist aesthetics in order to explore the politics of gender, sexuality, and identity. These include hybridization or the mixing of genres; metafiction, which comments on its own fictional status; self-reflexivity; intertextuality, in which the text draws on other texts; fantasy; pastiche; and irony. While postmodern devices are not in my view inherently radical, their use by Schulman facilitates the deconstruction of the narratives of (hetero)sexism and imperialism. Like many contemporary feminist novels, *Empathy* combines postmodern stylistics with a feminist critique of postmodernism, sharing its central theme with contemporary feminism: the possibilities of political solidarity and resistance in the postmodern world.

Sarah Schulman's *Empathy* gives a fictional treatment to many of these issues. The novel's theme is precisely that of feminism in the 1990s: the possibilities for political resistance across multiple and shifting identities. It asks the question of how we can empathize in a confusing postmodern world in a way that is politically and psychologically enabling. As such, it deals with the so-called big issues, thereby confounding the view that lesbian novels are particularist and lacking in general significance.

The novel operates a double gesture, deconstructing and simultaneously inscribing the political meanings of identities. It does this not in the 'add-on' manner of identity politics, but in a radically intersectional way, recognizing the 'multiple locations' of contemporary subjects. In the rest of the article, I want to discuss *Empathy*'s treatment of postmodernism and diversity in terms of four major critiques that it undertakes: a critique of the psychoanalytic theory of sexual difference; of heterosexism as implicated in women's subordination; of the politics of representation; and of ethnocentrism and American imperialism.

The themes of psychoanalysis – sexuality, identity, the unconscious, and psychic pain – are central to *Empathy*. The novel represents the psychoanalytic view of 'identity' as a kind of psychic violence which is based on the repression of unconscious desire. The aim of psychoanalysis, the novel reminds us, is to help people who suffer by listening to them through a form of empathy. The concept of transference, the psychoanalytic term for this, is integral to the cure. However, the novel highlights the historical role of psychoanalysis as a regulatory and normalizing technique with the aim of reconciling subjects to their 'correct' gender identity. It explores the psychoanalytic account of the acquisition of femininity which constructs female identity as lack, and asks 'how can I be a woman and still be happy?' Moreover, in focusing on lesbian identity, *Empathy* foregrounds the double erasure of the lesbian subject within a heterosexist society.

The novel's central tragi-comic conceit is that its lesbian protagonist Anna has never slept with another lesbian but always falls for ambivalent bisexuals. She can't understand why and so goes to Doc, apparently a pavement psychoanalyst who offers counseling sessions. In engaging psychoanalysis the text foregrounds its Jewish identity. It invokes and plays on notions of Jewishness, for example the stereotype that all New York Jews are in analysis or are themselves analysts or the children of analysts. Both Anna and Doc are the children of Jewish psychoanalysts, and therefore 'born' Freudians. There are obvious echoes of Sigmund Freud's (himself, of course, a Jew) relation to his female patients. Indeed, the novel represents a radical intertextual reworking of Freud's female case studies: Anna's lover in the novel is called Dora. Anna O. was Freud's first patient, Bertha Pappenheim, who with Breuer, invented the talking cure. Dora, whose real name was Ida Bauer, a resistant heroine for feminism, refused to name her desire for another woman and famously sacked Freud. There is also a character called Herr K, Dora's seducer in the Freudian case study, who Schulman rewrites as Doc's mentor and as 'a pioneer in the field of interruption theory.'

The novel's epigraph comes from Freud's 1920 essay 'The Psychogenesis of a Case of Homosexuality in a Woman' which defines female homosexuality as a combination of masculinity complex and frustrated desire to have a child by one's father. Freud states: 'She changed into a man and took her mother in place of her father as the object of her love.' This misogynistic and homophobic construction is internalized by the protagonist. As a result, Anna experiences extreme alienation from her body and sexuality and becomes a disembodied, dysphoric subject. Schulman represents her subjectivity through a correspondingly fragmented and discontinuous narrative style, split between the two protagonists, Anna and Doc. However, Doc rejects the sexism and heterosexism that inform psychoanalytic theory and, unlike Freud, he deconstructs the power relations of the analytical scene. He is aware both of the value of listening and the power it confers on the listener. Paradoxically, he himself has never been in therapy because he sees its potential for exploitation:

> You tell them one real thing and then the doctor thinks he knows you. He starts getting arrogant and over-familiar, making insulting suggestions left and right. You have to protest constantly just to set the record straight. Finally he makes offensive assumptions and throws them in your face. A stranger in a bar could do the same.

The novel undertakes a critique of the psychoanalytic theory of sexual difference, describing it as shoring up heterosexuality as a political institution. It articulates the lesbian feminist view that women's oppression is constructed in and through heterosexuality as well as gender. The text negotiates two main theories of lesbian identity, associated with the work of Monique Wittig and Judith Butler, two of the most influential theorists for lesbian feminism in the 1980s and 1990s.

In exploring the relationship between heterosexual women and lesbians, the novel addresses the issue of diversity within the women's movement. Despite the centrality of lesbians to so-called first and second wave feminism, lesbianism is commonly articulated as threat. The preferred feminist narrative of female solidarity is a non-sexual sisters-in-arms affair. Lesbians, as the novel shows, pose a challenging question: what happens when you eroticize relations between women? The sign lesbian works to detach gender from its assumed connection to heterosexuality. Lesbian difference thus complicates the concept of female identity. The novel uses this insight as a source of humor. At one point Anna remarks:

> Maybe that's the problem I've always had with female identification. It's like looking at Picasso's *Three Women* only to come away thinking, 'My breast is your thigh.'

It should be clear that *Empathy* articulates a postmodern politics of location, recognizing the fact that 'a person positions herself on quicksand.' In the course of the novel, Anna acknowledges the need for a new ethics, distinguishable both from the old overarching metanarratives and from politically quiescent models of postmodernity. She recognizes:

> that every single individual has to rethink morality for themselves and at the same time come to a newly negotiated social agreement. That's how Anna learned to be many people at once and live in different worlds of perception at the same time each day.

In subscribing to an ethical postmodernism, the novel rejects the politically disengaging mode of postmodernism, refusing the simulacrum, and insisting on the political meanings of identity and desire. It articulates a critique of postmodern relativism, of a world without depth, meaning, or value and demonstrates that postmodernism is a heterogeneous phenomenon, containing 'worlds of difference.' Schulman's text represents a symbolic exploration of women's unequal differences as articulated in contemporary feminist theory and in the process exhorts feminists to take seriously the possibilities for empathy as a political stance in a postmodern world of shifting locations.